© 2022 Ayodeji Olaifa

Edited by Amy Raynard

The Helper's Son
All rights reserved.

Paperback ISBN 978-1-7764020-5-2
Publishing Project by Bonani Contents
www.bonanicontents.com

AN AFRICAN NOVEL

THE HELPER'S SON

Exhilarating and suspenseful!
A story of race, culture and identity.

AYODEJI OLAIFA

DEDICATION

To Yety, Fikun and David.
Remember, I am because you are.

To my broader family, friends and acquaintances.
Thank you for the inspiration, your invaluable
support and for always cheering me on.

To anyone that may be caught in the web of an
identity crisis.
I hope you find meaning and a way to embrace your
uniqueness.

Ayodeji Olaifa
THE HELPER'S SON

Prologue

It all began with a toddler's cry.

The Johnsons were hosting friends for dinner. Everyone, including the little ones, had their hands full.

"Madam wants the house shiny like glass," Thembeka had told her friend on the phone earlier, as she apologised for not being able to chat for too long.

And without warning, a toddler's scream broke through the glass door, like thunder, jolting his mother out of her trance. "Oh, this child won't kill me," she mused as she raced towards the baby, dropping her napkin along the way. Thembeka slid the door open, scooping him up in a frenzy. She picked up his feeding bottle from the floor, wiped off the teat with her hands, and tucked it back into his mouth. She hoped that he would just go back to sleep. She desperately needed him to cooperate with her today. Thembeka hurriedly settled him back into his rocker, praying he would remain calm, as she rushed back to finish up in the living room. She still had the bathrooms to attend to.

However, he was relentless.

Just moments after his mother had put him down, the scream of 'mamma' would again reverberate around the house. Thembeka became very anxious. She didn't want Mrs Johnson to get livid again. She had complained the other day about the phone calls, and her baby. She thought she was getting too distracted at work and taking too long to complete her tasks. She had asked if there wasn't a relative that could help her with the baby during the week while she is at work. Thembeka had told her she didn't have any relatives in the city and her friend, whom they knew as well, had a full-time job. She was sorry about the inconvenience and had promised to work harder. She had also committed to working extra hours to make up for any lost time.

But all of that was now in jeopardy.

Thembeka swiftly rushed to the patio, trying desperately to pacify him. Normally, she would strap him on her back, which she suspected is what he desired right now, but there was a lot to do today. She didn't think 'backing him' was a good idea, especially if he didn't seem to want to sleep.

She gently tossed a 'borrowed' Mickey Mouse doll into his rocker, hoping that he would be engaged for a while, maybe even take a short nap while at it. It seemed to work as he smiled happily, clasping his tiny fingers around his mother's. Thembeka walked slowly back to the lounge, closing the sliding door behind her.

Again, the boy wouldn't stop wailing. His screams quickly drowned out the vacuum cleaner.

But before Thembeka could react, a different but equally demanding sound, caught her attention and that was of Mrs Johnson, who had come racing to the living room in a panic. The two women watched in absolute bewilderment, as a second baby on the other side of the door, banged on the sliding door without stopping.

Frightened by the clamorous sound of the banging, the toddler in the rocker suddenly stopped crying. He watched as a superior 'drama' unfolded. It was even more captivating when the tantrum came from the other toddler, on the other side. Mrs Johnson moved closer to her daughter, who continued to strike at the glass door with her tiny hands whilst rambling away excitedly in baby chants. Still rattled, Mrs Johnson opened the door. The daughter staggered on her tender feet towards the baby in the rocker, her friend.

She held out her tiny hands to the boy, and in the cutest way ever, attempted to hug him. She ended up hugging the rocker. Both women looked at each other, equal in stature at that moment, and too afraid to acknowledge what just happened. It only lasted a moment. The two women quickly reverted to the reality of their existence. One to the care of the two babies, as she tried figuring out how to manage the remaining chores, and the other for the more important task of ensuring there was enough wine and food for the guests.

But little did they know on that fateful day, that the universe had a different plan.

A plan that would change all their lives forever.

Part One

When Two Worlds Collide

———————

I t was 1992, the year everything changed.

Some say he was spooked by his name. But on this day, the sun shone powerfully through the beautiful Cape Town sky. It was going to be a good day, Jongikhaya thought to himself.

Tourists revelled in the grandeur of their newly found gem. South Africa had just opened to the world. The world came in droves to the land of Mandela, the newly freed hero, an iconic revolutionist. Oblivious to the plights of a country paralysed by the fear of retribution and drums of war, foreign tourists infested the country's beautiful coasts.

He watched as the 'ticket peddlers' hassled the tourists at the beautiful Victoria and Alfred (V&A) Waterfront covering a wide expanse of land in one of South Africa's wildest harbour – which opened just two years before Mandela was released from prison.

Several ferry businesses had developed in the city to take advantage of the new opportunity. Many were based at the V&A Waterfront, offering tourists (foreigners and locals alike) a trip of their lives, to see various marine lives – penguins, seals, dolphins, and various species of bird life – as well as the breath-taking views of the City Bowl, Table Bay, and Robben Island. There were rumours that Robben Island would be opening to tourists, who couldn't wait to set their feet on the island, a place that had been home to Mandela and many other struggle stalwarts for decades. He could imagine world leaders and celebrities lining up to take photographs on the island.

He had read in one of the weekend papers about an initiative aimed at auctioning 'A night in Mandela's cell' for some hundreds of thousands of US dollars. All aimed at world leaders, celebrities, and the affluent, that may be craving a night in Mandela's 'home' for eighteen years. Looking around him, with many tourists frolicking about, he agreed it was a great idea to capitalise on the momentum. There was an insatiable thirst for everything Mandela, providing ample opportunities for an industry to develop around the phenomenon. Even his mum was already talking about opening a Mandela soup kitchen in the township. It was not a bad idea at all. Maybe he could also think about setting up a guest house business on the island in the future, why not? He thought.

Except, the future was uncertain.

The political landscape had become even more heated in the period leading up to the country's first general elections. He had overheard his parents with some of their friends, talking about emigrating, just like his cousin had spoken about him and his friends moving into the 'white' suburbs. He had wondered if they intended on renting or buying properties there. In years past, such a 'revolutionary' statement would have resonated with him, but not anymore. He was no longer the hot-headed communist that thrived on controversies and intellectual dogmatism.

He feared that the climate in the country didn't seem as beautiful as the day's weather was.

Khaya (as he was fondly called) drained the rest of his drink, as he gazed at the beautiful sea. He always loved the sea view whenever he was out for coffee or dining at the V&A, especially today, when he knew it could be a long discussion. He was sure she would enjoy the vibe as well. A young African lady, one of the ticket peddlers, came over to him. Khaya knew it was only a matter of time before she summoned up courage. He had caught her eyeing him on several occasions – probably trying to figure out if he was a local or a tourist. "Hey," she began with an uncertain smile. Khaya smiled back at her invitingly. The lady closed in, just as he had hoped. She wanted to sell him a boat tour along the surrounding coastline, offering a breath-taking view of Granger Bay, Bantry Bay and Clifton, except that he wasn't a tourist, he told her. "Eish, askies," she apologised in a blend of IsiXhosa and Afrikaans, a reflection of the long history between the indigenous languages and those of the Dutch settlers. "No, it's okay" Khaya responded in English, as he often did. He was used to be an outsider. It's exactly how he had felt in the last few years.

From birth, Khaya found himself thrust into two worlds - distinct in every form, but also bound together like Siamese twins. He lived each day, torn between a life of his ancestors and another gifted by the generosity of humans. He strove to make sense of it all, even accept it, but the more he tried, the more it slipped from him. He would find himself living in the periphery of the two worlds, but not in any.

She needn't be sorry, Khaya had told the lady. He had always felt like a perpetual tourist in his own world, with home being only a figment of his imagination. The lady walked away quietly, unsure how to assist the young man. Time was money, and numbers mattered in her little world. She couldn't afford to waste any more time on a non-prospect.

Khaya looked at his watch again. He calculated she should be there in about thirty minutes and asked for a glass of water in the meantime.

He had booked a table for them for noon. Just

thinking about it makes his palm sweat in excitement. He couldn't wait to see the reaction on her face when he breaks the news to her. It would be priceless. She might even do a little dance routine, as she often did whenever she was overjoyed. He owed everything to her. Mammi never gave up on him, despite his rebellious behaviour. He still has all of her messages of love and encouragement. She even blamed herself for all his woes. How incredible she is. He smiled just thinking about her.

He had called the house earlier in the week to let his parents know he'd be visiting during the week. He had told them he had an important news to share. They were glad to hear from him, and they couldn't wait to see him again, his parents had responded.

Khaya was getting impatient. He looked at his watch again. This time, Mammi was running thirty minutes late. He thought it was unlike her to be late. She had always hated to be late for anything, preferring to wake up hours before an appointment to arrive early. "There is no excuse for lateness my boy," Mammi would always tell him. If he had known she would be taking this long, he would have gone to the house instead. *Could she have missed her way*, Khaya thought, as he looked anxiously from afar, into the crowd making their way to the Waterfront. He was sure she had been to the restaurant on many occasions herself.

Mammi knew the V&A inside and out. She had run errands for the Johnsons at the Waterfront all her adult life. She had also confessed to him in the past, how she had saved some of her wages for an evening at the Waterfront, often accompanied by her friend, Aunty Nosfundo, two indigenous African ladies, pretending to be rich and sophisticated, while getting super drunk.

It was during those times, that he wished the much-anticipated cellular service was already available to the public. It had the potential to change lives.

Khaya called out to the waiter. He needed to make a quick call, he told him as he rushed into the mall, praying that the telephone booths were still in good order unlike many on the streets. He was glad to hear the phone ring on the other side, as he waited impatiently for Mammi to pick up. She never did.

Thembeka stole a quick glance at the kitchen clock. She could still make it to him in time if she left now, she told herself, as she hurriedly stashed the remaining plates into the dishwasher, turning the wobbly knob to quick wash. She hated to have to work on weekends. She thought she heard a dog whimper. She listened again, but nothing. With so much noise from the machine, she couldn't be certain if it was the family dog whimpering or not. She had just checked on Leanne a few minutes ago,

11

and she was still in bed deeply asleep.

Thembeka dried the first batch of the washed plates with a napkin. She would have to take care of the rest of the dishes on Monday, she mused, as she hurried through the first batch.

Khaya had told her that he had great news to share with her when he called the house the day before. It's been long since she heard him sound so excited. She had tried all her motherly tricks to get him to spill the news, but he wouldn't budge. She had thought all through the night about the news, but more importantly about seeing him again after such a long time.

Suddenly, she heard a loud startling sound not far from the kitchen. It sounded like fireworks - only that it had a different chill to it. And in an instant, she realised it could be the sound of a gunshot. Her heart leapt out of her chest.

Moments later, the house phone rang continuously. Khaya had a bad feeling. He should go to the house, he decided, as he dashed by the restaurant to pick up his bill.

On the other side of town, in a small fishing village of Arniston, the Johnsons were having lunch on the terrace of their holiday home, when the housekeeper came to notify them of a phone call. They had left Cape Town on Friday for their holiday home, as they have been doing for the last five years. They planned to retire to the beautiful town in a few years.

"Is it Leanne?"Mrs Johnson asked the housekeeper. They were expecting their daughter to join them at the house. She hadn't felt good after lunch on Friday and had opted to stay back at the house in Cape Town when her parents left, promising to join them the next day, with her boyfriend.

Mrs Johnston had felt even more uncomfortable with the daughter alone in the house. As they drove out, they saw Khaya's cousin accompanied by a stranger, approach the house. She had never liked the cousin - ever since he had appeared in her house as a teenager, drunk and with the police on his heels. She had expressed her feelings to her husband on many occasions but would always dismiss it as nonsensical. The boy is technically 'family' he would say. "No madam, it's a man on the phone,"the housekeeper replied. Dr Johnson walked to the phone. It was a police officer from the Rondebosch Police Station.

They had bad news.

Groote Schuur hospital in Cape Town, renowned globally for its novel human-to-human heart transplant, but it was also where the young and athletic Kyle Johnson first set eyes on his future wife, Cindy Strydom. Cindy was a beautiful twenty-two-year-old Pathology resident at the Groote Schuur hospital. She caught the eye of many at the hospital, but her heart would only belong to one, the good-looking anaesthetist, Dr Kyle Johnson. He was a kind, caring and an extremely intelligent young man.

The child of a clergyman, Cindy was the third child and only girl of her parents. They were descendants of Dutch settlers, referred to as Afrikaners. Born and raised in Bloemfontein, a central part of South Africa, her parents moved to Paarl, an old town in the Western Cape, in the 40s when she was barely a year old, to take up a pastoral position in a church.

Kyle's parents were of Anglophone descent. They were second-generation British South Africans. His grandparents had immigrated to the Western Cape in the late 1800s, settling in the small town of Franschhoek, a town with a mix of the Dutch and French Huguenots, and one of the oldest towns in South Africa. Franschhoek boasts one of the most magnificent Cape Dutch architectures, while the French side of the town is renowned for its culinary excellence and some of the most beautiful wine valleys in the world.

In South Africa's settler capitalism, the Anglophone, or British Settlers, to which Kyle's parents belonged, were categorised as a more affluent and elitist category of White South Africans compared to the Afrikaners, who as a group in the early 30's grappled with widespread poverty. Thus, for a long time, the Afrikaners were considered in some quarters as 'poor whites', and inferior to the British White South Africans.

Kyle's parents were unhappy when he introduced the small-town Afrikaner lady, a fellow medical doctor, to them as his future wife in the summer of 1969. They had thought that it would be like one of his many relationships that had fizzled, so they never gave it much thought until now. The parents thought he could have done a lot better. Many British South Africans still loathed the Afrikaners for turning the country into a republic, ending the position of Queen Elizabeth as the Head of State. Kyle didn't share his parent's sentiments.

Doctors Cindy and Kyle got married the following year in Franschhoek – in a last-minute bid to appease Kyle's parents who had threatened not to attend the wedding. The newlyweds moved into a magnificent, four-bedroom house, with a small cottage at the back, in the quiet and prestigious suburb of Rondebosch in Cape Town.

When Cindy fell pregnant in 1970, a year after their wedding, she asked her mother to move in with her. It was a plot to ensure that her mother-in-law didn't move in instead. Their feeling for each other was mutual, but they managed to remain civil at the least.

Cindy had also recently let go of her domestic help. It was becoming increasingly difficult to get a 'non- radicalised' helper, in the face of the growing civil unrest in the country. Every black person she knew in the city either belonged to one resistant movement or another. Not that she could blame them, she had never understood the rationale for the government's 'apartness' policy. She remembered as a child, asking her parents if God hated the black people. "No baba, God loves everyone. No matter the colour," her father had told her. She grew up with those words taken to heart.

Cindy knew of a lady at Groote Schuur hospital. She was an African nurse who worked with her husband, Kyle. She asked Kyle to speak to the lady about a live-in domestic help. Perhaps she knew someone who would be interested.

Thembeka had been out of work for some months. She was down to her last penny and was tired of being harassed by the police each time she was in the city looking for a job without her dompas - a passbook. *It was unfair*, she thought to herself. *You are required to carry a pass to be in the city, but you could only have one when you get a job.*

She was getting desperate and worried that she may have to return to the homelands with her infant if the situation didn't get better. When a phone call from Nosfundo, her friend and roommate came, it ushered in a ray of sunshine. Nosfundo wanted to know if she would be willing to work as a live-in domestic worker. She told her that her bosses wife had just had a baby and was desperate to find someone dedicated to helping with the housework. She had told them that she might know of someone. Thembeka was overjoyed. Of course, she would be happy to take the job, she told her friend. "But I didn't tell him about Jonghikhaya," Nosfundo added. "I didn't want to scare them away."

"*Haibo*! What am I supposed to do with my child?" Thembeka reproached her friend, as they both mulled over an appropriate solution.

The Johnsons were immediately drawn to Thembeka.

She was young and energetic, clever and seemed to have little or no time for politics. She also communicated well in both English and Afrikaans. They agreed that she could take the weekend off.

Thembeka and Nosfundo had agreed to keep the existence of her child a secret from her employers. They found a neighbour that was willing to take care of the child during the day for a reasonable sum, while Nosfundo took over at night when she was off duty. The two friends were elated about the job. Nosfundo was glad that her friend would be less of a burden. It had been hard, living off her meagre income, all four of them – despite the little support she got from her own child's father.

She was truly happy for her friend. She wished the job would stick. It had been quite a ride for her since she left the Bantustans.

———

Born in 1953, in the Transkei, the homeland of the Xhosa people, all Thembeka ever wanted was to leave the *Bantustans* and their poverty for the bustling and affluent Kaapstad.

The homelands did not offer much to the average young black South African.

The youngest of three, and the only girl, Thembeka had always been different. She always had bigger dreams, and was never one to shy away from adventures. She had a reputation among the boys and girls alike in the village, as the '*umlilo*', the fiery one. Thembeka was drawn to the flamboyant.

As a little girl, she had been fascinated by tales from 'returnees' from the big cities, and stories about *abelungu* (white people). She particularly coveted the confidence and sophistication exuded by those 'returnees' from Cape Town. She thought they outclassed 'returnees' from nearby cities like East London or even farther off like Johannesburg, the city of Gold. There was just something different about the people of Kaapstad, she thought. Their aura and a sense of arrogance about them, she wanted it all - the array of designer clothes, shoes, a myriad of sunglasses, and even prescription glasses.

She relished the mouth gaping and rare sights of young Xhosa women driving cars – some even smoked like the *abelungu* women she had heard stories about. Thembeka longed for a time when she would swap her 'village looks' for the more 'sophisticated' city look. She already could imagine what she would wear on her first visit back to the village for Christmas.

But she didn't think she would be able to drive.

Maybe her father could have taught her, except, she never knew him. The only memories she had of him were anecdotal at best, if not complete fables. Her mother's version had stuck. Her father had 'absconded' for the city of gold, abandoning her mother and his three children to the mercy of the village. *Umkhulu* (grandfather) had told her that he had been spotted in Johannesburg and was rumoured to have remarried a Zulu woman who had born him two sons.

She resented him for abandoning them, and the city of gold, for swallowing him. She vowed never to set foot in the venomous city and never to marry.

The only man she ever loved was *Umkhulu*.

Her grandfather was the only father figure she knew. He was always protective of her. He indulged her truancy, and never hesitated to make long treks to get her enrolled in new schools, whenever she was expelled from an old one. *Umkhulu* wanted her to be a teacher. He would always joke with her that the reason she struggled so much with schooling was because the witches knew how great of a teacher she would become, and so they would do anything to thwart her efforts.

Whenever they saw an *impundulu (the Hamerkop, a bird believed to be associated with witchcraft)* on the way to school, her grandfather would insist that they kill the bird, spending minutes, sometimes hours in the process. Thembeka wondered years after, if she had succeeded in killing an *impundulu*, maybe things would have turned out differently for her.

Thembeka's mother worked far away from the village. She and her brothers never saw her much. She remembered *Umkhulu* had been very angry on an occasion when they had all visited her mother at her house in a neighbouring town where she worked as a shop attendant. Her mother, who had not expected them, was home with her boyfriend, both visibly drunk. She had been upset with *Umkhulu* for bringing her children 'uninvitedly' and didn't want them to stay. *Umkhulu* had vowed never to look for her again. Thembeka's mother never visited the village since the incident. There were rumours of her alcohol problems and subsequent destitution. After battling a long illness, Thembeka would later hear that she had died of chronic liver disease.

She never mourned her.

Thembeka was now the surviving matriarch of the family. *Makhulu* (grandmother), had passed on when she was little. She remembered her as being less indulgent of her, unlike her grandfather, but she was a strong woman. She had a farm where she spent most of her time, toiling to feed her family, while grandpa's bicycle shop remained only a promise - it never did break through.

When she was sixteen, Thembeka dropped out of school. She no longer wanted to be a teacher. She had never wanted to be one and worried that it would break *Mkhulu's* heart. Maybe she should have killed the *impundulu*, Thembeka thought to herself sarcastically. Her grandfather was disappointed but was not surprised. He had always suspected that the relationship between her and school was not going to last long. She could barely keep herself in school and out of trouble, long enough to benefit from school. Her teachers had tried hard to motivate her – thinking there was a spark somewhere in her. He had, however, hoped that she would finish Matric (High school).

Thembeka had dreams bigger than the village. She only wanted to go to the big city like her friend, Nosfundo, who had gone to Cape Town to become a nurse. Nosfundo had told her of black people living like *abelungu* (white people) in Cape Town. They had good jobs, drove big cars, and lived in big houses. She wanted to live like that too, and only by leaving the homeland, could she hope to achieve her dreams.

Nosfundo and Thembeka grew up together in the village. Their mothers had been good friends and neighbours. They considered each other as family.

Slightly older and less fiery, Nosfundo got along

well with Thembeka as kids in the village, until she left for Cape Town to attend nursing school. They only saw each other whenever she visited the village - usually during the festive periods – and would spend hours, often into the late nights, talking about the big city.

———

With the meagre savings from working part-time at her grandfather's bicycle shop, and the extras he had stashed in her bag, Thembeka arrived in Cape Town at the end of the year 1969, with only a name and an address on a paper that she stored in her bag.

A rural girl in a big city, she stood out like a sore thumb in the hustle and bustle of the bus park.

Thembeka found some Xhosa taxi drivers who offered to help her locate her friend. She lost half of her money to their shenanigans but was glad when she was finally reunited with her friend in Gugulethu township - one of the designated habitats for indigenous African people who worked in the city (the city was a place reserved exclusively for white people).

A month had passed since arriving in Cape Town, and Thembeka had yet to find a job. She was impatient. She accompanied her friend to the city on numerous occasions, joining the hundreds of black people who flooded the city in search of jobs, and at the mercy of the apartheid police who demanded their passbooks.

She was beginning to wonder if there was any iota of truth, whatsoever, to her friend's stories about the big city. She had been surprised when she arrived at her friend's house, and even more disillusioned as the days turned into weeks without any hopes of her realising her dreams.

But the universe did offer some hope after all.

Thembeka found a cleaning job at a nearby clinic in the township. She was glad she could now start saving some money to get her own house and send some money home to *Umkhulu*. She missed home a lot. She missed *Umkhulu*, her brothers and her friends. She missed the familiarity of her home compared to the strangeness and detachment of the township. She started to write short memos to her grandfather, detailing some of her experiences in the big city, as a way to manage the loneliness she was feeling.

One of her memos was about the cost of living in the township. She complained to her grandfather that life was very expensive in the township. Many of the things that they bought in the township, cost twice the price in the city. But it was expensive and risky going to the city, she wrote. Her friend had also increased her share of the house bills – she felt that the bills should have been split into three. It was unfair that she had to pick up half of the bills, even though her friend's two-year-old constituted part of the household. She ended with some good news. She was planning on going back to school to finish her matric.

The job at the clinic helped Thembeka settle quickly into her new community. She made new friends and 'admirers' in the community.

Thembeka and Nosfundo were a popular pair in the community, especially with their umbrellas that shielded them not only from the rain but also from the blazing heat of the summer months. They quickly got accustomed to the sneers and jeers from young men and older ones alike, who mocked them each time they walked the streets with their umbrellas. Some would call out to Thembeka, mocking her about her dark skin, and how it was the sun that needed shielding from her adumbral skin.

While in the past, she would have confronted the men in her true character, but ever since Nosfundo had scolded her, she knows to just keep walking, occasionally cracking a smile at one or two that she thought were good looking or cocky in some weirdly funny way.

Trouble, they say comes in threes.

Thembeka's troubles started at home. She had received messages from her grandfather, requesting financial support. The summer rainstorm had destroyed many properties in the village. They were lucky to have survived with minimum damage, only the house roof was impacted and needed to be repaired urgently before the next storm. Thembeka didn't have enough money to spare. She had to borrow from Nosfundo, who had grudgingly obliged to her. She had reminded her of her outstanding debts, leading to a war of words between them.

Soon after that, her supervisor at the clinic called her in, just as she arrived for her morning shift. The clinic was underfunded and could no longer afford to pay many of its non-essential staff. They would have to reduce her hours to manage the payroll. Thembeka was distraught. She was hoping to settle her numerous debts that month - she hadn't been happy with the way things were since their last fight over money. She may have to find a second job, she thought to herself, without any premonition of what was to come.

But indeed, when it rained, it poured.

Just when Thembeka thought things couldn't get any tougher, she would soon be catapulted into a devastating and life-changing situation.

Just after midnight on a fateful Saturday, Thembeka and Nosfundo were returning home from their friend's 21st birthday party, on the other side of the township. There was nothing unusual about the night, except that Thembeka had again, had a little too much to drink. It was a habit that continually irritated Nosfundo. She worried about her friend who never seemed to know her alcohol limit. Whenever they were out, Nosfundo was always the sober one, the one to fight off opportunists— drunken men who were always out to take advantage of her. "Sometimes, I just want to get sloshed too," she had told her out of frustration on many occasions.

On this particular day, Nosfundo was not as sober as she would have loved to be. Her friend was already out of control at the party, and sharks already smelling blood. She told herself it was time to leave. In her drunken state, she grabbed her friend's arm, dragging her out of the house, as she protested. The two drunken ladies, staggered along the poorly lit street, yelling, and singing, as they made their way home. She had to pick Thembeka up from the floor several times, to get back on her feet. It was not a pretty sight.

Out of the darkness, company suddenly appeared.

Three men watched with sinister interest, as the ladies sang and danced drunkenly on the road, moving from one end of the road to another. The men saw an opportunity. One of them walked up to the ladies.

As he approached, Thembeka looked straight at him in the darkness. All she could see was the shadow of a man, but she thought there was something vaguely familiar about him. She giggled drunkenly. The man grabbed Thembeka's hand, and gestured with a nod, for his friends to join the party. Nosfundo sensed danger.

She tried to pull her friend out of the man's grip, but Thembeka had already slumped to the floor. Nosfundo looked across the road, to the other men. She noticed that one of them was hesitant, and the other made his way toward them.

Something in her wanted to scream at that moment for help, but for some reason, nothing came out. She saw her friend on the floor, pulling at the man, who stood looking down at her, as she fondled herself and teased the man, asking him to make out with her right there. Immediately, the other man who had crossed over the street grabbed Nosfundo's hand. She yelled at him, and at her friend. She wanted to run as fast as her legs could take her, when the man suddenly tightened his grip, and with a voice that sent chills down her spine, told her to shut up or he was going to cut her. He pulled out, what looked like a knife, to Nosfundo in the dark. The third man had now joined his mate. Trembling uncontrollably with fear, Nosfundo watched, as the distance crept in between them, as her friend was being assaulted, knowing the same fate awaited her.

The two friends were discovered at different times, by separate parties. Nosfundo had been abandoned in a dilapidated and empty 'shack' by her assaulter. She was found by community members who had been alerted of the heinous crime, shortly after Thembeka was discovered in the early hours of the morning, by friends leaving from the party. They had found her sprawled on the floor, naked, and completely passed out. She had been immediately taken to a nearby clinic, oblivious to the events of the night. She had remembered being with Nosfundo at the party.

Members of the community suspected the worst and immediately set out on a search mission for her friend, and within an hour, had found her unconscious in a 'shack'. The police were called to the scene and she was immediately taken on the back of the police van to a nearby clinic. Some of the community members recognised her as a nurse who worked in the city.

———

Her period had never been late, until now.

Thembeka had taken an over-the-counter medication the moment she realised she was missing her menstrual period. The medication was prescribed by one of her co-workers at the clinic. Her period was a few months late.

She had been too scared to bring up the subject with her friend, Nosfundo. Her co-worker had assured her that everything would be fine. It was something they all used at the slightest suspicion of something going amiss. But when the sickly feeling persisted, despite all the medications she took for influenza, she decided to visit her local clinic.

She stood there, frozen for a second and incapable of any thoughts, as the nurse broke the news to her.

The nurse asked if she was okay. She would have

to register for the prenatal classes, the nurse added. As she heard the nurse mention the word 'prenatal', the impact of the news began to sink in. She remembered a saying in her culture, *that when you have fought hard not to be shamed but was unsuccessful, you then start to fight not to die.*

At that moment, Thembeka felt death was the better option.

She had thought nothing could be worse than the trauma of being raped, but here she was, having to deal with the worst news of her life. The most deplorable seed imaginable, growing in her belly.

Suddenly, she started to gasp, as the tears streamed down her cheeks uncontrollably. The nurse rose quickly to her assistance and led her to a waiting room, where she laid down. She was having shallow breaths and feeling quite faint. The nurse insisted that they would have to keep her under observation for a few hours before she could be allowed to go home.

Her life had fallen apart. She was in a dark hole.

She cried bitterly and cursed the day she came to the city. She wanted *Umkhulu*. She wanted to go back home to her village and never return. She cried some more, as she remembered the day her life turned upside down.

Thembeka and Nosfundo barely spoke about the night.

All she had were pieces put together from Nosfundo's statement to the police and vague recollections of the night. She thought it was funny how the brain arbitrarily manages how one recollects certain traumatic and gruesome events. She was grateful for the scanty recollections, unlike Nosfundo, who had to bear the brunt of her full recollections.

The night had created a rift between them. She had a feeling that Nosfundo resented her for everything that happened. But it's fine, she blamed herself for it anyway.

She smelled the men every day, and still had nightmares. It hurt, even more, knowing that she couldn't share her pain with anyone else. It wasn't something that one discusses publicly. It was taboo. She only had her friend, but she could tell how much she was also hurting.

The police had offered them therapy but all she wanted was just justice, which by all indications, wasn't forthcoming. It had been months since the incident and no breakthrough yet.

They had both thrown themselves into their work.

Nosfundo worked double shifts, anything to keep

her away from the house, from her friend and the memory of the night. She had sent her son back to his father. While Thembaka continued with her cleaning job at the clinic. She spent most of her free time kicking herself and crying out her eyes in her memos to *Umkhulu*.

But it all changed with the news.

The pregnancy brought them together again. Thembeka had gone to the city to see her friend as soon as she was discharged by the nurse. She desperately needed someone to talk to. Nosfundo was heartbroken at the news of her friend's pregnancy. All the emotions she had been suppressing, came rushing through, as she cried hysterically. It was the first time they had both confronted the emotions of the night. Thembeka's pregnancy was fraught with despair.

Just a few months into her pregnancy, she got word from home that *Umkhulu* had passed away after a slight illness. Thembeka had no more tears left to shed. Unlike her, *Umkhulu* lived his dream. He was content and was happy to meet his ancestors.

She had written about her rape ordeal in her last memo. She was too ashamed to see him, even if he was dead. She was too ashamed to go home, defiled and carrying a 'cursed' baby in her womb.

She lit a candle for him and held a private prayer for his soul. She was sorry she disappointed him. Thembeka cried as she watched the candle burn out, in the corner of her room.

—————

Tears rolled down Thembeka's cheeks as the nurse handed her the newborn baby. He was born on 12 April 1971. Thembeka watched in the fullness of joy, as her baby suckled for the first time, marking a new beginning in the mother and son relationship and an embracement of her reality. In a whisper, she named him, *Jongikhaya*.

She repeated the name to herself, surprised at the choice of name. It wasn't a name she would ordinarily have given to her child. It had popped up in her head a the moment, as she looked into his fresh and puffy eyes, while he suckled. But what was even weirder than the choice of name, was the sensation she felt, the moment she whispered the name. She had a feeling that a force bigger than her, had orchestrated the moment. It just felt right that the 'unwanted child' would be the custodian of her home. Even though he was conceived in agony, she hoped that he would be a source of joy, the one to heal and bring people together.

Thembeka was happy the rift between her, and her friend had been repaired since the news of the pregnancy and got even better with the birth of her baby. They had promised to be each other's strength. The two friends even joined a local community coalition against sexual abuse in the township.

Thembeka continued to work short shifts at the clinic while she hoped for something better. She worried that her friend was overwhelmed by the bills. Thembeka again, was desperate to find a second job, except there were a few opportunities open to a nursing mother who was also uneducated.

One Sunday afternoon, as Thembeka set about doing laundry, she watched in dismay as the heavens opened, and the rains poured heavily. It was a sun shower. The sun stubbornly shone through the heavy rain. It was a sign of a good omen, she told Jonghikhaya, who had just turned one. The infant was disinterested in her mythology. All he wanted to do was creep and crawl towards the older kids who were running around in the rain topless. Thembeka wouldn't have any of it. He had been snotty since birth, and she was beginning to worry if he'd ever have a dry nose.

Later that night as mother and son prepared

for bed, she heard some movement by the door. Alarmed, Thembeka rushed up from the bed. It was Nosfundo. She was only expected home the next morning but had cut her shift short. She needed to share some news with Thembaka.

Nosfundo may have found another job for her friend. One of her bosses at work needed a domestic worker urgently. It would have to be a live-in, Nosfundo had told her.

Thembeka cried out in joy, waking up her child in the excitement. She remembered the sun shower earlier, as she clasped her mouth with her hands, jumping up and down in joy. She hugged her friend and thanked her for always looking out for them. She was ready to start immediately, she told Nosfundo. Except there was a problem, Nosfundo didn't think it would work out if she showed up with Jonghikhaya. Thembeka found an elderly neighbour, who agreed to care for the child during the week, while Nosfundo volunteered to step in at night. She would swap her night shifts with her colleagues, she assured her.

And thus, began the life with the Johnsons.

The Johnsons were impressed by Thembeka's dedication to her work. Mrs Johnson, who had taken extended maternity leave, to be with her toddler, was particularly glad to have found someone who seemed very reliable and less interested in all the political agitations that engulfed the country. Thembeka was equally happy with her job and her new employers. The arrangement with Jonghikhaya was working well.

Until very early one morning, when Nosfundo had visited Thembeka at the house - her workplace. Thembeka had been surprised to see her. Her friend rarely visited her at work. She immediately suspected something was wrong. She was right. Nosfundo told her Jonghikahya had taken ill overnight. He had been nauseous. Nosfundo had cared for him all night, and taken him to the clinic the next morning, where he was being kept under observation. Thembeka had immediately asked Mrs Johnson for the day off, which eventually turned into three days off. She had sent messages through her friend to her boss, Dr Johnson, letting them know that she had a family emergency. Thembeka learnt that her child had suffered a bacterial infection and was put on antibiotics treatment.

She was in a dilemma, even though his fever had subsided, he was still very clingy, and she didn't think she could return him to the care of the neighbour, feeling the way he was. Nor did she think she could continue to stay off work any longer. She asked Nosfundo for help.

On the fourth day, Thembeka showed up at work with Jonghikhaya firmly straddled on her back, to the bewilderment of her employers. Mrs Johnson had reluctantly agreed to let her keep the child at work, but under the condition that it wouldn't distract from her work. Thembeka was relieved, and so was Nosfundo. It seemed it had all worked out after all.

Every day of the week, Jonghikahya watched his mother, sometimes from the comfort of her back and other times, solitarily behind the glass door, in the rocker provided by Mrs Johnson.

He also longed to play with the other child in the house, whom he had seen on a few occasions crawl around the house, and sometimes to her mother. Even though his little mind was yet to comprehend the complexities of the human calendar, he looked forward to the weekends with his mother - in a different environment, with no restraints, and with people who laughed all the time. Then, one morning as Jonghikhaya settled into his rocker, everything changed.

Mrs Johnson had repeatedly complained about Thembeka 'backing' her child while she worked. She didn't think it made her efficient. She had observed her taking multiple breaks to attend to the child, who often kicked his mother, forcing her to take him off and on her back frequently. Mrs Johnson requested that the child be kept on the patio when she worked. Thembeka had successfully coped with the new arrangement for a week when Jonghikaya started with his tantrums. For some reason, he refused to be left alone on the patio. His incessant screams for mamma would soon become a big irritation for everyone, including the little Miss Johnson, who for a while, had been wondering what game the other baby was engaged in behind the huge glass door.

Little Miss Johnson took matters into her hands that fateful day. She had heard his scream once again, and with her wobbly little legs, had staggered to the door. Pressing her face onto the glass door, she looked him in the eye, cracking a little smile from the other side of the world, while babbling away inaudibly. And like a child under a spell, she banged on the door with as much energy as her feeble hands could muster, startling both her mother and Thembeka in the process.

That was the last time that Jonghikhaya stayed at the patio.

The two infants became inseparable. Little Miss Johnson would not let him out of her sight except when she was asleep or during weekends when he was away with his mother.

Jonghikhaya grew up as a member of the Johnson household.

The Johnson's fought tooth and nail, to make sure that he attended the same school with their daughter, Leanne. These were mostly schools that were reserved for whites The Johnsons were dissenters, insisting that their black child attend 'whites only' schools. They felt it was their way of protesting against the repressive system.

In time, Khaya—as his friends called him—would learn to call his biological mother, 'Mammi', and his adopted parents, 'mother and father', or at other times, 'dad and mum'. While it may have seemed to be mere semantics to his developing mind at the time, but with time, Khaya would be caught in the webs of his two worlds as they unfolded.

The inherent contradictions of which, would come to shape the rest of his life. As is always the case at the onset, Khaya enjoyed a colourful childhood, much to the envy of his cousin and other black friends. From growing up in the serene and opulent part of the city, and running around on a well-manicured lawn in his home in the suburbs, where he learnt to swim at the early age of four, to the weekend encounters in the dusty and rusty Gugulethu township - where, with his cousin, he mastered how to navigate his way between the alleys of the small houses and 'shacks', Khaya didn't know any better. His extended family consisted of a mix of indigenous African family, many of whom he had never met, Afrikaners and English family from his adopted family. In many instances, he was either the only 'black' one in the crowd or the only 'white' in the group, depending on which side of his family tree he found himself.

Indeed, there were many perks to his colourful life.

Khaya learnt to speak multiple languages. His mother only spoke to him in isiXhosa, her native language, while he picked up English and Afrikaans naturally at home, with the Johnsons, and in school. He could have secret chats in isiXhosa with the 'aunties' at school who cleaned, when he was feeling unhappy and alone on the school playgrounds because the white kids refused to play with him. He relished the looks on their faces, as they experienced, perhaps for the first time in their lives, what it meant to feel isolated.

He also enjoyed it when the kids in the townships asked him endless questions about the city and the white people. They had heard many stories about his big house, the big trees, and the river (swimming pool) in the house, from his cousin, aunty Nosfundo's son. He enjoyed the embellishments, as he watched their eyes widen in total amazement. They didn't like their dirt roads very much - his cousin had tried to make him understand. They would rather be in the suburbs, splashing around in the pool - even if they couldn't swim - and playing hide and seek in his beautiful tree house that looked much more fanciful than the abandoned shelters in the township.

It was a reality that he grappled with as a child.

As a little child, he had never understood why his cousin, whenever he visited with his mum, would kick and cry, refusing to leave when it was time. However, as he grew older, and as he listened to the other kids in the township express their desire to visit his house, he realised he had some form of leverage, which he surely exploited to gain many friends in the township.

It was the curious looks whenever he showed up at school with his white sister, Leanne, and his white parents, or during family vacations to grandpa and grandma in Franschhoek, when his white cousins either refusing to come close or tried to rub off the dark paste off his skin, that occupied his growing mind.

He often felt uncomfortable, on the rare occasions, when Mammi accompanied them on such trips, or to school. While he was happy to see the curious looks on the faces of some of the people fade away, as soon as they saw Mammi with the rest of the family, they immediately connected the dots. It was always a challenge, that often left him feeling ashamed, picking between Mammi and his mother in public spaces. It didn't help that Mammi still had to work and care for everyone, even when they were out and about as a family.

Khaya had always understood that Mammi was a domestic worker. He understood that she worked for his parents, the Johnsons, and had eagerly repeated the story of his adoption as told by Mammi, to the cleaning ladies at school and anyone else curious enough to ask. Mammi was grateful for the Johnsons love towards her and her child. She was happy that her son would have a fair shot at a different and better future compared to many who roamed the streets in the township with no hope. But she was also troubled that her son was being raised differently. She had made sure that they only spoke isiXhosa whenever they were alone. She encouraged him to spend more time with his black cousin and friends in the township. Mammi pleaded with her friend to visit the house more frequently with her son so that they could get closer.

Khaya loved his cousin a lot. They grew very fond of each other. While Khaya taught him how to swim, he taught Khaya how to be street smart, and how to speak the 'township' lingo. But Khaya's parents didn't feel the same way. They thought the cousin was discourteous and was a lot of trouble.

Khaya would learn to manage these complexities privately.

Yet, accepting the realities, when juxtaposed in the public was not always pleasant. His life was in truth, fraught with many paradoxes. These two worlds, great privilege and poverty, would come to be a dominant source of internal conflict as he grew up. The ordinarily simple things became complicated as he found himself trapped in both worlds but belonging to none. It also didn't help that he didn't know anything about his father.

Khaya had always wondered about his biological father. As a child, Mammi had told him that he had two fathers. Mr Johnson being one and the other was his biological father, the one that looked like him. Khaya had been confused. He requested for photographs of his father, but never saw one. Mammi had told him how cameras were not readily available at the time, and how the ordinary people couldn't afford to take photographs.

As his curiosity peaked, Mammi would point to different men at different times who looked like his real father. It soon appeared that, his biological father, looked like every black man in the township.

Mammi and aunty Nosfundo had both told him that his biological father had abandoned him at birth and had disappeared without a trace. When Khaya asked about his biological father's family, he was told he had no family. He had been raised in an orphanage, which had unfortunately gone up in flames, many years before Mammi met his biological father.

Khaya thought something was amiss. But couldn't figure out what was.

He had asked his mum and dad about it, if they knew anything about his biological father. They also couldn't assist, and it appeared, they didn't like it much whenever he brought up the subject. Mammi would also scold him for asking questions. She wanted him to let go and show a bit more gratitude. "You have all the family you'll ever need," she would say in rebuke, while adding that Dr Johnson was a better father than his biological father could ever be. Khaya didn't want to upset Mammi or his parents. He just wanted to know a bit more about his biological father, he would reassure her.

Like a little child presented with yet another pet, Khaya was elated, when a few years later, just as he turned thirteen, Mammi started dating.

Thembeka had met Khwezi in Gugulethu, on one of her weekends off in the township. Nosfundo and herself had become actively involved in a community coalition against sexual abuse. They attended meetings every Saturday afternoon, a few minutes' walk from their house. As the two women made their way to the meeting under the scorching afternoon heat, they noticed a man approach them with a giant umbrella in hand. With a broad nervous smile, he asked the women if he could provide them with some shade, as he flipped opened his umbrella with the skill of a ringmaster in a street circus. The ladies smiled. Even though Thembeka thought he could have done better, she was nonetheless flattered. Thembeka remembered him as one of the better-looking men who always chattered, whenever her and Nosfundo walked to the taxi stop with their umbrellas. She nudged her friend playfully, "I wonder why it took him so long to muster up the courage," she whispered.

Khwezi walked the ladies to the meeting, intermittently wiping off sweat from his burning face, as he made small talks. He promised to see the ladies again as they bade him farewell. His eyes locked with Thembeka's eyes as they both looked back to check each other out.

Like Thembeka, Khwezi was born in the homelands. He moved to Cape Town in the 60's in search of work and lived in Gugulethu. Unlike, Thembeka, Khwezi completed high school. He managed to get a job at the city's harbour as a dock worker, loading and offloading cargo.

Khwezi had set his eyes on Thembeka from the first time he saw her at the taxi park in the city. He had hoped to talk to her on the taxi, but unfortunately, she had sat in the front passenger seat, with the driver. Khwezi could only find a seat at the back of the taxi. He had helped her out from the back when she struggled with the fares. It was obvious that she was new to the city and unaware of the taxi norms. It was customary for the passenger in the front seat, not only to assist in collecting the fares, but also to ensure that the accounting was right. But as soon as they got to Gugulethu, Thembeka had disappeared long before Khwezi could make it out from the back of the taxi.

He would later see her and her friend on several occasions in the township. He had tried, but unsuccessfully, to get her attention until the fateful day, when the weather presented a rare opportunity.

Khaya liked Khwezi.

He was someone he could pretend to be his biological father, someone who truly looked like him. Khaya was always happy to see him on weekends when they were in the township. He confided in him a lot and even built up and imagined them becoming a true black family - Mammi and Khwezi getting married someday and having children. He fantasised about having other siblings that looked like him.

These thoughts occupied Khaya's mind when he started to become overtly conscious of his colour.

Adolescent meant the peak of the resistant movement and the gradual roll back of many of the Apartheid laws in South Africa. It was a period characterised by rising protests as many blacks flooded the cities in search of jobs. During this time, many schools that had been reserved for whites only, started to admit an increasing number of black students. Khaya's parents thought it best that he attends one of the new boarding schools with a relatively higher number of black students. They acknowledged that it was essential for his mental development that he attended a mixed-race school. He had struggled emotionally through elementary school. They hoped that the new school would provide him a platform to openly express his identity.

It did exactly that. Maybe more than what the Johnsons had anticipated.

Khaya's two worlds collided in high school. It was the time when his fragile mind became a fertile ground for extensive radicalisation and resentments.

At school, Khaya interacted with people of all races. While the teachers were all white and most of the students too, Khaya didn't feel that the issue of colour was a dominant theme on campus. However, he found that his blackness was accentuated in public spaces, where blacks were still not allowed. Bus drivers, train attendants, waiters at restaurants, police officers and other adults, advertently and otherwise, forced him to identify with his colour. In time, he would become accustomed to his shifting consciousness, knowing when he was 'white' and when he was 'black'.

Khaya drew closer to Khwezi as he longed for a different identity. Over the years, Khwezi developed drinking problems. He had lost his job at the harbour and sought to find comfort in 'the bottles'. He became more and more frustrated, picking up short term domestic jobs now and then in the city.

In the summer of 1989, Thembeka introduced him to the Johnsons, who were looking for a replacement for their gardener. Khaya was glad when he came home from school one evening, to find him working in the garden, as Zoe, Leanne's puppy, but actually the family dog as Khaya preferred to call him, tormented him by digging multiple holes around the garden with its tiny paws.

The two grew even closer, spending days in the garden at the house, and weekends together in the township.

Khwezi was equally fond of him—and Zoe. He provided additional tutoring on the history of the African National Congress and taught him a few tricks on gardening. Khwezi thought he had a knack for gardening and thought he should become a horticulturist. The Johnson's had a magnificent garden which has benefitted from many gifted hands in the past, but none cared as much as Khwezi.

He introduced new exotic plants and built an entire new bed of herbal plants in a secluded area of the garden. Khaya's mum boasted of his genius additions to her culinary during dinner parties. He truly loved working with the soil and could also easily have been a successful horticulturist if he wanted to or rather, but only if he could stay sober long enough, to be one.

Khaya was aware of Khwezi's drinking habits.

He had joined him on several occasions at the 'shebeen'—a local township pub, incurring Mammi's wrath each time. Khaya was unaware of the depth of the problem.

Mammi had moved in with Khwezi in the township. Khaya would stay with his cousin at aunty Nosfundo's place whenever he was in the township, while Mammi would go straight to Khwezi.

Khaya was oblivious to the abuse. Mammi was careful to keep it away from him. It was a huge shock when Khaya found out that Khwezi had turned against his mother.

Khaya had walked in during an argument.

Just as he approached the door to the house, he could hear a drunk Khwezi shouting at Mammi. He accused her of selling her child to white people, the same people who hated them. Khaya could hear Mammi yelling back at him. She screamed that the same people he claimed hated them, had loved her and her child, gave her a job when no one would, and offered his lazy and drunken self, a job. "You should be grateful to the bosses," Mammi yelled, just as Khaya opened the door, and confronted the man who had just hit his mother.

Things got worse between the two lovers and weekends became more toxic. Mammi moved back to her friend's place but stayed in the abusive relationship—much to Khaya's disdain.

Khaya was grateful for school. He avoided spending time with Khwezi whenever he was home but was worried about Mammi. He hoped for her sake, that she would end the relationship. It was not a surprise when he learnt that his dad had fired the gardener.

His dad had found out about his drinking problems, and his lackadaisical attitude towards work. They had also discovered—after a much delayed background check— that he had been involved in a few cases of domestic violence and petty theft. They had to let him go. Khaya wished Mammi would also let him go but she continued to shield him.

He knew things were getting dangerously out of hand. Mammi was troubled, and he thought she was better without him. He didn't want things to degenerate further. He thought it was ironic that, someone, who advocated against domestic violence, would subject herself to it. It was akin to his own struggle – the continuous shifting of his consciousness that left him feeling trapped most of the time.

———

1990 was a significant year for Khaya.

It was the year that Nelson Mandela was released from prison after serving 27 years. It was a moment equalled to none in the history of the country. Blacks of all shades across the world, celebrated the dawn of a new beginning and whites reflected on the past as they mulled a new way forward in the new South Africa. The electric sense of jubilation felt across the nation would mask the fragility of the moment at least for another year or two. It was also the year Khaya gained admission to the University of Cape Town (UCT), one of the few universities in 'White South Africa' that admitted a few black students, for a bachelor's degree in African Politics.

Over the years, Khaya had become radicalised. He had joined a number of black student-organisations in high school, travelling across the country to mobilise fellow black students to join the revolution—aimed largely at pressuring the Nationalist Party to release Nelson Mandela and other struggle Stalwarts.

He was immediately 'inducted' into the 'Hall of Fame' of radical black students at UCT as soon as he stepped foot onto the campus. Khaya and his cohorts consumed Leninist and Marxist doctrines with an insatiable appetite. They built up deep hatred for the status quo—which meant everything associated with the whites, including white businesses and wealth. Khaya and his fellow radicals envisioned a new South Africa where the poor black miners took over the wealth of the country under a black majority rule.

It was admirable. Except that he had a white family and lived in a white house with white privileges. With time, these feelings would evolve into a deeper identity crisis.

It was particularly conflicting for him, coming to terms with the fact that, the same people that showed him love could also be responsible for the many hardships inflicted on his kind. Increasingly, it became hard for him to come back home to a family who looked like his 'oppressors'. He began to stay away from home, choosing to live on campus with friends, even during school breaks, and spending less time with his sister on campus.

He also resented his black family. They reminded him of his contradictions. He resented Mammi for his circumstances, and for continually subjugating herself to the 'bosses'. He resented his ancestors for being weak and succumbing easily to the settlers.

It was a pain to be around him, the conscious black man, as his sister often called him.

He was embroiled in frequent outbursts and

fights on campus and cherished long and often, contentious debates, with fellow students and lecturers on matters of race, politics, and economic liberation.

As a leading member of UCT's Black Student Council, Khaya travelled the length and breadth of the country, organising and mobilising support for the coming general election. His parents worried about his commitment to his academic work. He resisted any interference from them. Mammi was equally troubled. She sensed her son's detachment.

They fought more frequently than they used to. He no longer wanted to spend time with her and would hide under one excuse or another. He had even suggested that she quit working for his parents. "They don't really need you anymore," he had argued. He wanted her to set up her own retail business in the township. "We are taking back the country," he told her.

His relationship with Leanne was not spared either.

She took a lot of strain. She was close to him. They had been inseparable growing up. They had fought each other's battles, ditching friends without hesitation, if any came between them. She was used to the fights, the cheekiness and childish meanness. But she couldn't make sense of the anger and the resentment he now exuded. "He now spoke differently," Leanne had told Mammi on another occasion when she had asked about him from her. She had thought it funny when he told her it was the 'revolutionary speak'. She had told him he sounded very rural and uneducated, which infuriated him further. He insisted it was the 'struggle diction', which once didn't have credibility, if one couldn't speak like that, like Mandela and others did.

Leanne was petrified. "How brainwashed can you get," she had lambasted him. She reminded him that he didn't even know anything about his heritage, and for someone who had never visited his village, it was rich trying to be 'the people', she jibed. Leanne wished that things could go back to how it used to be. That he would come home more regularly and be the sweet little brother she loved and missed so much. Yes, she may not have fully understood the complexities of what he had to deal with, but she was a part of it too, she had told him. She grew up defending herself and her family from friends and mischief-makers who in many instances, had questioned her about her parent's motives. They were a family bonded together in love. Their parents were hurting and so was Mammi. They all missed their Khaya.

But they had all missed a big part of his problems. Khaya longed for acceptance.

He wanted to be 'fully black'. He yearned to be accepted within the 'black circle' without having to carry the baggage of being a 'coconut'—black outside and white inside.

He didn't have any difficulties with other Africans, as a matter of fact, some of his closest allies were fellow black students from other African countries. His closest friend at the university was an older student from Nigeria.

But when it came to his own people, fellow black South Africans, he struggled to find acceptance. He was deemed not 'black enough'. Even his cousin never took him seriously. He thought he was just being spoilt and seeking attention. He admonished him for turning against his parents who showed him love as a black child, even when it was a crime to do so.

However, Khaya saw things differently. For starters, he surely didn't feel 'white enough'.

As he spent the bulk of his time overcompensating, turning himself into a jerk at home and at school, he would end up paying the ultimate price.

Khaya and the rest of the Black Student Council were implicated in a vicious assault on a group of white students at their residence. With mounting pressure on the University, the Black Student

Council was disbanded and all its executive members, including Khaya, were suspended from the school.

———

Khaya froze.

He watched from the rare seat of the cab, the flashing blue lights of police cars and ambulances that were sprawled across the road leading to the house. He knew something tragic had happened.

He was too scared to disembark.

The black taxi driver asked nervously if that was the address. He probably didn't want anything to do with the police - Khaya couldn't blame him. Things were very tense in the country. But Khaya feared something bigger than the police at that instant. He stepped out of the vehicle and made his way to the gate.

The gate was wide open. Khaya walked inside. He identified himself to the two officers who had immediately accosted him on sight. Just as he was asking the officers what was going on, and that he wanted to go inside the house, some of the neighbours walked in.

The gave him a hug and mumbled some words he couldn't understand. He hurried to get inside the house, but his feet wouldn't let him.

Another policeman came up to him. He asked if Khaya could wait. There was a break- in, the officer started to say, as Khaya rushed into the house. He saw traces of blood on the door path leading to the living room. By then, more officers appeared from inside of the house. They held him back as he became more frantic. They made him sit down. Khaya could see more officers outside in the yard. The neighbours looked distraught and spoke in muffled voices.

One of the officers told him that they had been called to the house by neighbours who had heard gun shots earlier in the morning. Upon arrival, they had found two women, fatally shot. One had died on the scene, and the other had been rushed to a nearby hospital, she was in a critical condition.

Khaya's world was spinning out of control. "Mammi!" He cried out, just as the officers in the yard, rushed to stop a car driving through the gate. Khaya looked out into the yard. It was his parents that had just arrived.

The officers told them that Thembeka had been

rushed to the Rondebosch Hospital.

She had lost a lot of blood and remained in coma after two successive surgeries. The doctors didn't think she'd make it. Khaya joined Mammie at the hospital. He never left her side. He held on firmly to her hand, scared that if he let go, she would drift away. He prayed every minute that God must spare her life.

However, Thembeka succumbed to her injuries the second day.

Khaya was left in tatters. He felt every part of him had been violently ripped apart!

He had failed his mother again, in her last moment. Khaya sobbed uncontrollably. He had wanted her to be happy, to tell her about the scholarship. To show her that he had finally got it back together.

But it wasn't to be.

It was as if he could hear his mother's last thoughts, as she turned towards the sound of the gun shot, the moment she came face to face with her worst nightmare. She knew in that instant, that she'd never get to hear what her son wanted to tell her.

Thembeka looked through the mask, into the eye of the shooter, as she muttered a short prayer for Khaya before the bullet hit.

Part Two

Across The Bridge

——————

Khaya looked out from his window seat, as the airplane taxied. It was his first time travelling outside of the country. In another time, under a different circumstance, such an endeavour would have attracted all the bells and whistles.

"Excuse me, sir. Please kindly fasten your seat belt," a crew member interrupted his thoughts. He switched off his phone and tucked it away in the seat pocket opposite him as the aircraft disappeared into the clouds—leaving behind all the sorrow and heartaches of what seemed like an eternity.

His mind drifted...

The house was a crime scene. The professional cleaners had done a great job getting rid of the red stains, but the smell of death and sadness hung heavy in the house. Police officers came in and out at will. Khaya and his parents remained, but each one completely immersed in the misery of the moment. They were like strangers in the house. Nothing could be normal again.

Khaya had always known that his mother didn't like his cousin much. She had complained severally to him and Thembeka about the boy and his group of friends. She didn't want him visiting her home with the friends, and thought they were a bad influence on Khaya. He had disagreed. He thought his mother was being unreasonable and might even be prejudiced. But when she accused him of the crime, Khaya thought she had gone too far. It was one thing to dislike a bunch of kids for being truants, but another to accuse them of such a gruesome crime, khaya blurted out to his parents. These were normal kids, who just happen to look different and act differently. He could understand that everyone was hurting.

He had just lost Mammi and his sister too but that didn't give them the right to throw around accusations. Why would his cousin, who was practically like a sibling be involved in Mammi's death? Khaya asked in anger. It just didn't make sense to him. He wanted his dad, who hadn't said a word the entire time he had been arguing with his mum, to intervene and make her see his point of view, but the dad wouldn't say a word. He was too heartbroken. Khaya was certain he was crying the entire time.

He could hear his mum from the living room. She was glued to the investigating officer and almost seemed like she was hoarding him. She was shouting at the officer again. She demanded an arrest. She was adamant that Khaya's cousin be arrested and was upset that she had to teach them their job. She repeated to the officers that the boy had visited their house with two other strangers the day before the incident, asking for their son,

Khaya. She was sure they had something to do with the death of her child. She was inconsolable.

The investigating officer was accustomed to grieving families, and their behavioural patterns. He was patient and showed great understanding in his conduct to his mother and the rest of them as a matter of fact. It was a very difficult time for everyone.

They cooperated with the officers as best as they could, even when they requested to have another team come over for additional fingerprints, days after the break-in. Khaya went up to the investigating officer. He wanted to know if there were any leads—besides his cousin. He thought there had to be something, maybe the neighbours saw something, he asked the officer. They had some CCTV footage from their neighbour, the officer had informed him. However, they were still busy with the analysis and would share the findings with the family as soon as possible. He warned Khaya not to be overly optimistic, he didn't think there was much that could assist them in their investigation, from his preliminary analysis of the footage. The neighbour's camera was not of good quality and the footage was captured in monogram. The criminals had worn facemasks, but there was always the chance that the family might be able to recognise the body shapes or movements. Again, he promised to provide a detailed report as soon as the team was done with the footage.

Khaya stepped outside of the house. Some of the officers remained in the parked van. The perpetrators need not worry. No one was on their heels it seemed. Khaya shared his mother's frustrations—at least the part about having to teach the officers their job. It seemed the police would rather spend time questioning the family than actually going out to find the criminals who killed Mammi and his sister. He kicked at the brick fence, unleashing his frustration while the officers watched in muted sympathy.

Khaya arrived at John F. Kennedy International Airport in the early hours of the morning, completely wrecked.

He had been kept awake all through the night flight by the sonorous snores of his fellow passenger. He had felt bad after vigorously shaking him in a bid to end the opera but to no avail. Maybe the poor guy was just tired and needed the deep sleep, or maybe he had a medical condition that made him sing. Khaya apologised to the sleeping man and pushed his ear plugs even deeper into his ears, hoping for some respite.

Anxious about the new endeavour, he was glad when he heard the pilot announce the descend to

JFK Airport. He looked out through the window. A new world awaited him somewhere beneath the clouds. He closed his eyes as the tires hit the ground with a big impact, sending a loud vibration across the entire aircraft. Khaya joined the little kids on board in a round of applause for the landing, more out of relief rather than approval.

A sudden sense of helplessness enveloped him as he disembarked. He walked closely behind the other passenger hoping that somehow, they were all headed the same way, while at the same time, keeping his eyes on the airport signage showing 'Baggage Claim' and 'Passport Control'.

After a long walk, they made it into a huge arrival hall, with immigration officers directing the passengers to different sides of the queue. Khaya made his way to the queue designated for 'Non-US Residents'. At the end of the queue, a female immigration officer directed him to a row of self-help screens. She had moved to the next traveller before Khaya could ask for more information. He walked over to a vacant screen. After a few minutes of fiddling with the system, he eventually figured out how to input his information, and scan his passport. He picked up the printed sheet with a barcode and was again, directed to another queue. He could see several officers in booths. It was where one had to get your passport stamped.

The queue moved very fast. He hadn't observed any drama like those he had seen on border control shows on television back home. He became a little nervous, nonetheless. "Next!" An officer in a booth beckoned to him. He quickly walked over to the booth. "Hello, where are you headed?" The white officer asked, as he reached out for his documents. "Florida, sorry, Orlando," said Khaya nervously. The officer didn't seem to notice. He kept staring at his passport. "How do you say your name?" The officer asked, without raising his head. "Jonghikhaya. Jonghikhaya Johnson," he responded. Now the officer looked up. Khaya was well accustomed to that reaction, especially from non- Africans. It was a look that said as politely as possible, what the heck does that mean?

The officer didn't bother trying to pronounce it. Rather, he simply asked what the name meant. Khaya told him it meant 'the custodian'—the one who watches over the home. "Uh, huh," the officer muttered, as he requested for additional documents. Khaya handed him the rest of his admission documents. To his relief, the officer asked for his fingerprints, and then stamped his passport. He asked how Mandela was doing and welcomed him to the United States of America. "Be quick to return home," he added with a hint of sarcasm, as he waved him on.

Bayo waited anxiously in the arrival lounge. He had just checked the flight information screen for the umpteenth time. The flight status still read 'Flight delayed' on the screen. He walked to a café nearby to get himself a cup of coffee. He can only hope that the flight was not cancelled.

Khaya thought about his parents. Maybe he should get a local phone, he thought to himself, as he looked around the waiting area for his connecting flight to Orlando, Florida.

Cellular phones had just been introduced to the public at home, and everyone had been rushing to get one. He had also gotten one just before leaving for the States. He wanted to inform his friend of the delayed flight and also his parents. He hadn't been able to let them know that he had arrived in New York.

None of the shops could help him. Unlike in South Africa, the phones in the USA were somewhat linked to each individual state, the attendant had told him. Khaya was confused. Perhaps it was best that he waited to reconnect with his friend before making any purchases, he told himself, as he walked away, wondering why getting a phone was so complicated.

The boarding gate was suddenly vacant. Khaya wondered if the flight had been cancelled. One of the airline staff called out to him and asked if he was on the flight to Orlando. The passengers had all boarded and they were now making the final boarding call. Khaya doubled up, presented his ticket, and quickly made his way to the aircraft. "Oops, that was close," he said to himself, as he settled into his middle seat.

The flight to Orlando was uneventful. He fell asleep as soon as they were in the sky and only opened his eyes some few minutes to landing.

He had to get up for a passenger who needed to use the restroom.

Khaya looked out the window as the plane touched ground. He was fascinated to see that they were in the middle of a busy road. The plane taxied along an extensive overpass, built above a major highway in the city. *What an engineering genius*, he thought, as he watched cars and trucks speed by underneath the bridge. It was no doubt it was a prefect entry into a city of magic.

Khaya followed Bayo's arrival instructions. A short ride on the airport tram took him from one end of the arrival terminal to baggage claim, where Bayo would be waiting. He hoped he was still waiting, despite the long delay. Indeed. He was. Khaya saw him first. He had not changed much since their university days. He still had his athletic build but for some reason looked a little taller now. Maybe he was the one who had grown shorter, Khaya thought to himself.

"Hey, Bafana!" shouted Bayo, as soon as he spotted him. Khaya smiled.

He was now stuck with the name. Bayo had first heard the name earlier in the year when the newly re-admitted South African team participated in the African Cup of Nations under the name "Bafana Bafana". He had called Khaya to tease him about the name and had since bestowed the name on his dear friend from Bafana land.

Bayo would always carry a torch for the country. He had been one of the few black students—and probably even one of the fewer African students— at the University of Cape Town in the late 80's and early 90's. His parents had sent him to South Africa to complete his studies. Nigerian school system was crippled under military dictatorships in the 80's and 90's—strikes and school closures were rampant.

Those who could afford it sent their kids outside of the country to complete their education. Bayo found himself at the University of Cape Town, which apart from being one of the best universities internationally, had also built a reputation for itself as an institution opposed to apartheid.

The University was nicknamed, "Moscow on the Hill", during this period because of its anti-apartheid stance. The University of Cape Town was admitting black students, albeit in small numbers, as far back as the 20's.

"Who are you calling Bafana?" Khaya pretended to throw him a punch. He was happy to see him again.

The drive to the city was as magical as the plane taxiing on a city bridge. Khaya grinned like a little child as they drove into the city. Everywhere he looked, there was a familiar sign directing you to Disney World's Magical Express. This was every kid's dream, no matter which part of the world they live. It was no different with him. As a kid, he had asked Santa for a visit to Disney Land for his 10th birthday. He only got a ticket to Gold Reef City instead —a local entertainment park- and a scolding from Mammi afterwards. She had discovered his letter on the Christmas tree in the main house and had taken a peek. He remembered going to her apartment one afternoon after school, and Mammi being very angry at him. She had been disappointed in him for making such an outlandish request. All attempts by Khaya to make her understand that Santa was capable of making all dreams come true, didn't succeed. She thought he was watching too much fantasy TV and blurted out in anger that Santa didn't exist at all. If he did, there wouldn't be any poor and hungry kids in the world. It broke his little heart when she told him Christmas presents are bought by the adults.

Such was the nature of their relationship growing up; one lived in a fairy land, and another in the real world. She always made sure to remind him of his true identity, something that confused him even more. How he missed her so much. But here he was... in Orlando, Disney Land as a disinterested grown up, no thanks to Mammi- who had succeeded in ridding his mind of all fairy tales.

As they continued their drive on Lake Buena Vista Avenue, Khaya couldn't help asking his friend how it felt, living in one of the most popular cities in the world? "A huge burden," Bayo responded, without hesitation. It occurred to Khaya that this was not the first time he had been asked the question. "My house has become a guest house to families and friends— and even strangers referred by friends," Khaya laughed. That was typical Bayo, never one to hide his feelings.

Life is filled with contradictions. One moment you are flying high with the birds and the next moment, it seemed like the air is being sucked out of your lungs.

He was lucky to have received a scholarship from the Black Excellence Foundation to study in the

United States of America. Not many people are lucky to get a new lease on life.

He was sure it had taken all of his parent's prayers to get him out of the self-dug hole back at home. Just when he thought he was back on the right track, life grabbed from him, the only thing that kept him going. He remembered how happy he was when he heard about the scholarship. He was more excited for Mammi than for himself. He had stayed up all night imagining the look on her face, and her celebration dance when he showed her the letter.

It would remain only in his imagination.

Khaya resolved to make the second opportunity count. He hoped to move beyond the pain and the sadness of the moment and embrace what the future held. *He had failed her once, he wouldn't fail her again*, Khaya said to himself.

The University of Florida in Gainesville was some distance from Orlando where he stayed with his friend. He had erroneously picked the school, thinking it was the same one that Bayo had attended. It was too late when he learnt that he attended Florida State University in Tallahassee instead. The framed master's degree certificate in Nuclear Engineering, hung proudly on his living room wall.

Bayo volunteered to drive him to Gainesville. One of his earliest observations was that everyone drove in the States, and they lived far from everything—the shops, offices, schools etc. Maybe they did not mind the distance, or maybe they had gotten used to it. For Khaya, the two hour drive from Orlando was a stretch coming from a country where there was a shopping mall for every street, and people usually lived closer to work—at least not an hour away in free-flowing traffic like the case in the States. Khaya was intrigued.

It felt odd driving on the 'wrong side of the road', but it was a good experience. Bayo had stopped mid-way into the trip and asked if he wanted to drive. Thankfully, he had remembered to bring his international driver's licence along with him.

He never really liked driving long distance, but the excitement of his first drive on American road, took care of any inhibitions he had. He drove into the busy campus at noon. Besides the fright he got at the school's intersection when he thought an oncoming car was driving straight into him, the rest of the drive was a breeze. *Maybe he could get his own car, he joked.*

Khaya went straight to his one o'clock appointment with his program officer. He hoped to complete a few administrative tasks on the first day, while

Bayo proceeded to another end of the campus to meet up with an old friend, whom Khaya would later find out to be his ex- girlfriend. Khaya felt less guilt knowing there was at least an additional consideration for his generous offer to take the day off work.

He would travel by bus for the rest of his time at the University, often falling asleep on the bus both ways.

The realities of life in America hit him hard and fast.

While he was grateful for his friend's kindness and hospitality—which provided a soft landing for him in the new country—he was nevertheless overwhelmed by the ballooning living expenses. He never would have thought that finding additional funding to augment his scholarship was going to be such a challenge.

He had left South Africa with less than five hundred dollars. The bulk of his savings having gone towards his travel ticket, it didn't help when the embassy had insisted that he should buy a return ticket. But not that any of it mattered anyway, he would have gladly left for anywhere else with an empty pocket, if need be, given the circumstances back then. Anywhere would have been better than staying home, grief-stricken.

Except that he couldn't escape the bills that bore down on him in the new country. He stared again at a rumpled piece of paper on the table. He had worked out his monthly living expense. He had agreed with Bayo to split the rent and groceries with him. It was only fair that he carried his own weight, given it was his decision to stay far away from his university campus.

The idea of sharing an apartment with a stranger closer to school just didn't appeal to him, even though that may have easily saved him a fair amount, on the cost of a monthly pass from Orlando to Gainesville.

Another option would have been to ask his parents for support. *He hadn't asked them for money in a long time, he recalled.* Their relationship had been severed since he dropped out of school and even more so now, given the way he had departed the country, he didn't think there was a chance they'd be sending a cheque. He didn't want a cheque either. He was better off without them. He would have to make it work one way or another, he reassured himself. All non-essentials would just have to wait until he was able to get a part-time work on campus.

His program officer had sounded optimistic that he could get a temporary position on campus. There were a few students who worked in the library and school cafeteria. He was sure he'd be able to get something, albeit within the limits of his study permit. He might even get lucky with some external organisations that provided funding to international students, the program officer added. It was good news to Khaya. The last thing he wanted was to be distracted so early in his studies with financial matters.

Khaya grew up seeing Mammi care for others. He didn't think he would have to do the same.

Two months after arriving in the States, Bayo introduced him to his former agency, The Seniors Care Group, it was called. Bayo was a caregiver for more than a year. He had needed the wages to support himself through school as well. *It was what most foreign students and immigrants did on the side, he had told him.* More importantly, it was a tedious job. But if he embraced the opportunity, he could quickly find it exciting. *No patient is the same,* Bayo had said, as he prepared him for the task ahead.

In the fall of 1993, Khaya applied to the agency as a part-time worker.

On his first day at work, he took the eight o'clock bus to the agency. He had been requested to report to the office that morning. He could feel the weather was starting to get colder—not much different from

Cape Town's winter months, except it didn't rain as much. *He would have to layer up a little more,* he reminded himself, as he waited impatiently for the bus to arrive. When the bus eventually arrived, a few minutes after schedule, Khaya couldn't help but notice that it was unusually empty for that time of the morning. It seemed that the recent delay in the bus's schedule, must have left some passengers disgruntled and forced to make alternative plans. Only, there weren't many alternatives. He could understand why many Americans, like back home, resort to driving their personal cars.

He reported to the receptionist as soon as he arrived at the agency. She had looked at a giant clock behind her desk the moment Khaya walked in, insinuating that he was late for his training. Khaya resisted the urge to try and explain his lateness to her instead, he asked to see the manager. She offered him a seat in the waiting room. "The manager wouldn't be in for another thirty minutes," she said. "So much for her 'being late' attitude," Khaya mumbled to himself, as he joined a host of other newbies in the room, all waiting for the manager.

Khaya introduced himself to the group. He looked around at the mix of diverse caregivers. Majority were Hispanics—men and women that seemed to be in their 30's. There were a few Africans too, mostly older women, one was quite elderly, making him wonder how she'd cope with the job. He thought the Africans in the group looked West Africans, but he wasn't sure. Bayo had told him to refrain from assuming that everyone who looked a particular way was West African. He had told him that there were many West Indies people, as well as African Americans, that could easily pass as West African migrants. He decided to stick to the younger group, he would be Hispanic for the day.

He overhead some of the other groups discussing wages. He remembered Bayo had told him that the earnings were standardised, and he didn't think there was much room for individual negotiations. Most of the agencies paid the minimum wage. The working hours were also capped, partly because the agencies didn't want to pay overtime and because the job itself was stressful. They were obliged to manage employee burnouts from both, physical and emotional stress. Khaya also learnt that caregivers who coveted more earnings, like him, often applied to a second agency for additional hours. It was also not unusual for some clients to demand for more time from a particular caregiver that they really liked.

Kegan arrived an hour later. He was accompanied by a lady, whom he introduced to the group as the training coordinator. The group was directed into a bigger room with better heating. Each one was asked to go to a photo booth. They were to input their personal data and have their photograph taken. He heard some rumblings among the group, it was from the older African women—they would soon disappear from the group, and from the room. He would later confirm with Bayo that the women probably disappeared because they didn't want their photographs and fingerprints matched to the 'working permit details', they may have purchased *under the table.*

Khaya pushed the 'submit' button on the machine before him, and seconds after, he retrieved a paper identification card. He folded it into a badge and inserted it into a plastic cover provided. They were instructed to have it on whenever they visited the office or were at a client's house. He moved to the next room, where Kegan conducted a quick interview with the group.

When it came to his turn, Kegan asked about his experience working with the elderly as he had mentioned in his application. He was advised to do so from Bayo. He had told him to come up with some random experience taking care of his sickly grandparents back home. Kegan wanted to know the nature of the care he provided. Khaya rambled through it. All he could visualise was Mammi helping in and around the house, but Kegan didn't seem to have noticed his ramblings. He moved on to the issue of his study visa, and the permissible working hours. Khaya assured him that he was fully aware of the restrictions, and he had already worked out how to manage the shifts. Kegan seemed happy.

The rest of the training was straightforward. He had to do some computer based caregiving courses in addition to the regular general hygiene and equipment handling training, conducted by the agency staff. The online training included courses on Dementia, Infection Control, Alzheimer's, CPR, Basic Life Support and Communication skills, among others.

He was done with both the online courses and the office training in just under five hours. They were told that they would receive a full shift's (eight hours) wages, thankfully.

Kegan came into the room just as he was rounding up for the day. He had great news. He wanted to know if he was up for an immediate assignment. The agency had just received a request from a client, whose account they have been chasing for a while, for a three-day live-in shift. The client's regular caregiver had an emergency and had to travel. Kegan reckoned since he was the only one in the group with some care experience, he'd be best to take the case.

The case was the care of a senior with dementia. Kegan promised to send more details in an electronic case file later that day. Khaya hadn't expected to start work so soon. He was delighted. It seemed like his money trouble was about to become history. "Thank you very much," Khaya said and stood up to shake Kegan's hands, as he made his way out of the office.

Khaya was up before his alarm the next morning.

He went over his prepacked work bag once again. He couldn't afford to leave anything behind. It was three-day live-in assignment. He also went through the client's portal on the agency's caregivers app, which he had downloaded the previous night.

Kegan had confirmed that the client will be providing two meals a day, which was more than enough for him, he didn't have to worry about cooking his own meals. Khaya had calculated that the journey to the client's house would take about one and a half hours by bus (two connections). Kegan had emphasised the importance of being early. The client's wife loathed being late for her hair and beauty appointments.

They had agreed to meet at the client's front gate. Kegan had apologised for not able to give Khaya a lift to the client's place. *He had to run some errands before making his way to the client's place,* he said.

They agreed to meet at the client's house at eight am. The house was located in Winter Park, one of the most expensive suburbs in Florida and arguably in the entire country.

Located just few miles outside of the city, the beautiful trees forming an alcove along the streets—the trees reminded him of his home in the Southern Suburbs of Cape Town. It was indeed a very beautiful house, standing taller than most of its neighbours with elegant high stairs, leading to one of the biggest and beautifully crafted porches he has ever seen. The porch overlooked a lake, which he had been told housed some of the most ferocious alligators in the city.

Khaya waited at the client's gigantic gate, unsure whether to press the buzzer or wait for Kegan. He knew from experience that no one was allowed to loiter around such streets, but he didn't have to wait long. Kegan arrived at the client's house ten minutes before schedule. The gates suddenly swung open. His suspicions had been confirmed. Whoever was inside had been waiting for Kegan to arrive before letting him in.

Side by side, they climbed the long stairs to the porch. It felt like the entrance to a giant cathedral. Kegan pressed a bell on the elegant wooden security front door. A tall, beautifully dressed woman, who looked like she was in her early sixties, opened the huge door, to welcome them in. The words of Kegan kept ringing in his ears as they walked in, *"Caya, this is a big client. We have to keep him happy".*

Kegan introduced them. Again, pronouncing his name 'Caya' like most Americans did, he gave a big speech about him being a scholarship student from South Africa and studying at the University of Florida. He told the woman that they were lucky to have him as he's had ample experience back home taking care of many of his sickly relatives.

The woman showed little interest in the speech. She was visibly in a rush to get to her hair appointment. She was in the middle of telling Kegan that they were happy that he could get someone in such a short notice, when they were interrupted by a younger woman. Khaya couldn't tell from her appearance if she was related to the older woman.

Kegan introduced her as the woman's daughter. The daughter asked some additional questions, and asked, to her mother's chagrin, if they could have a quick demonstration with the client. Kegan immediately responded, "Of course, 'Caya' would be happy to," as the ladies led the way to the client's room a few meters away from the living area.

He was in a wheelchair. The wife quickly introduced Khaya as the temporary caregiver. The client was aloof. They asked if Khaya could help him get up from the wheelchair to his walker.

He was on pins and needles. He could feel his palms getting sweaty and his heart started to pump so fast, he thought he would pass out.

It was the same feeling he had the first time he had tried talking to a girl in high school, except this was felt ten times worse. The client looked at him a little groggily, as he approached. Trying hard to ignore the anxieties, and the blazing eyes around him, Khaya moved in closer.

The previous day's communication training came in handy. Khaya smiled to the client, introduced himself again, and told the client that he would be helping him get up now into his walker. The stillness in the room could be cut with a knife as they watched him attempt the impossible.

It was a dismal failure!

It took all four of them to get the client into his walker. The client's wife was furious. Kegan was completely red-faced, while the client's daughter looked like she had just recovered from a bad fit.

Obviously, all the right skills were not used. He had never had to help anyone get up from a wheelchair, nor into a walker. He was drenched in sweat and completely embarrassed. The client's wife was livid and asked Kegan with a raised voice if the caregiver was at all competent.

She didn't think he could care for her husband. But for some reason, one that Khaya would never know, she decided to let him stay. Yes, they were desperate for someone to be there until their regular caregiver returned, and the daughter was too shaken to have any opinion. She just looked on still standing by her father's walker.

It was a miracle that he was still standing in the room.

As he was being shown to his suite, Kegan, the pragmatist, could only hope that he would work harder at winning the family's trust, and be retained as their 'fill in'. Khaya was sure that he would never strap his work experience story from the onset again. *He must be used to all sorts of dramas and embellishments from job seekers*, Khaya imagined.

Khaya promised him that he would do everything within his power to win them over, as he walked him out to the front door. Khaya remained in the house for the next three days. Swimming and sinking, but had managed to stay afloat by the end of the third day.

In time, Khaya would become accustomed to the

equipment—including the highly automated recliner chair—and general patient handling.

Mrs Smith, as he had come to know the client's wife, still watched him like a hawk, whenever she was not out on her numerous beauty treatment appointments. His shifts had become more regular and had increased to include some weekends, whenever the Venezuelan lady was away. Kegan had been reluctant to allocate more hours to him, but he had eventually given in. Khaya needed the extra wages more than ever.

He was closer to Mr Smith. He soon found out that he was not the aloof person he thought he was when they first met. In fact, he was quite friendly and can be talkative—with a flair for some humour too. He was particularly interested in law and politics and chatted a lot about South African politics.

Like the rest of the world, he was elated that Nelson Mandela had been freed from prison after 27 years and wanted to know what his prospects were of becoming the first black president of the country. He had thought that it would be better if Mandela abstained from politics in its entirety, to enjoy his hard-won freedom, especially now that he was an old man. But on the other hand, he also agreed with Khaya that, if anyone could deliver on the promise of emancipation for black South Africans, and transformation of the society as a whole, it was Mandela. He had the political capital that would be required to rebuild the nation.

Mr Smith often complimented Khaya on his good grammar. It was his experience with many other Americans. It seemed that the majority of immigrants or caregivers, that they were exposed to, were from non-English speaking countries.

They also chatted about other topics. Khaya enjoyed their conversations about sport as well. He was an ardent fan of football—American football. Khaya loved rugby and soccer, and together, they would talk at length about their favourite teams and all-time sport heroes. The National Championship Playoffs were the highlights of their time together. He rooted for the Kentucky College Team, which was his alma mater and ranked 18th nationally. The Florida Gators were his next favourite, but they would always break his heart.

But none of the conversations survived into the following day. They would start afresh each new day because of his acute dementia. Khaya was saddened by it. He could imagine how difficult it must be for the client and his family, to have to suffer from memory loss. It was all new and disheartening for him. In some ways, it helped the client to see life from a fresh perspective each time.

Simone, the client's daughter also dropped in frequently. She was the only child and an attorney, just like her father. It didn't take Khaya long to figure out how tightly knit the two were, judging by the way the father lights up whenever she was in the house. They chatted a lot about the family business. The father wanted her to move back to Florida to take over the management of his law firm. The discussions always ended up in more technical matters of law. She always sought his opinion on cases she was handling. Khaya always tried to give them some privacy whenever she was around, but she'd insist that he stayed each time. She didn't seem to be bothered by his presence.

They didn't talk much, except when she wanted to quiz him about his background, family and all. Khaya was livid when out of the blue, she took out her phone and snapped his picture. When Khaya objected, she argued it was for safety reasons. Khaya reported the incident to the agency. He thought she was wrong to take his picture without his consent. But other than that, they went along just fine.

Her relationship with her mother was different. She was stoic. It was similar to the relationship his late sister, Leanne, had with his mother. The two butted heads until the last moment. While her mother was fiery, Simone was the cool-headed one.

She intervened on his behalf on several occasions, when her mother had let off on him for not doing certain things properly.

Mrs Smith was beautiful and had a strong personality: passionate, confident, and forthright. Khaya admitted to feeling intimidated around her. *She couldn't be more different to her husband,* he thought. It was her intensity that attracted her to him. Mr Smith would later narrate the story of how he met his wife as a sixteen-year-old blonde in the small town of Idstein in Hesse, Germany.

Dick, as he was known in his younger days, had been a member of the US troops in Germany during the Second World War. In his mid-twenties, and with his father's forestry and logging business in distress, as a result of the great depression of the 30's, young Dick enlisted in military service during WWII, and was soon deployed to the US military base in Berlin.

On a routine visit by some of the allied forces during the occupation, to the Schloss, a temporary military hospital in Idstein, Dick noticed a very attractive young lady, who worked in the hospital's cafeteria. She was exceptionally beautiful and tall. He also noticed how she stood tall among the officers. Most other women, and older, tip-toed around the occupation army often with their heads bowed. But this lady didn't. She was defiant and needed no help in handling the unwanted advances and misconducts of the officers towards her. She also spoke a little English.

He had gone up to her on one of the days. He asked if she could give him a tour of the city. He was willing to pay her for the service. Almut had looked at him in the eye, as if trying to sniff if he was a jerk or not. To his surprise, she obliged. She would choose the day and time and demanded to be paid up front. He was also to show up in civilian clothes.

Dick was smitten.

They would make many more of such tours around the country for the next four years that he was in Berlin, until he was drafted back home in 1951. He was thirty-four. Almut had just turned twenty, and heartbroken.

Dick kept his words. He wrote daily memos and would send them out to post every weekend. She wrote back to him, describing how she walked in expectation, every two weeks, to the only post office in the town to pick up his letters. The postmaster had come to recognise his letters. He would always separate the letters from others and keep it neatly in his office for her to pick up. He wanted to know if she would be leaving to join him in America.

They got married in Louisville, Kentucky two years later. Dick had taken over his father's logging business and managed to turn it into a successful business. He was also a year into law school when they got married.

It was January 1994. The 'snowbirds' had brought with them a bit of the northern chill.

Khaya shivered at the bus stop with his hands tucked away in his coat. He had bought a pair of leather gloves from Macy's, the other day, but when Bayo had laughed at him, he decided to hide it. He wished he had hidden them in the pocket of his coat instead.

He moved closer to the crowd, hoping to get warmer. The bus was late again. It was his second week at the new shift. Kegan had called him late in December about a new case. It was for a female senior with a bad case of dementia. They needed someone for the weekdays. There was a lady, who stayed during the weekends.

He had met Melinda the week before. She was Mexican and in her late thirties but looked at least ten years older. Melinda had sent him a phone message the previous night asking if he could come in a little early. She had to get to an interview and didn't want to be late.

Khaya reluctantly pulled out his hand from his pocket to take another look at his watch—a painful exercise in the excruciating cold. The bus was annoyingly late. He had to make an alternative plan. He stepped away from the crowd, brought out his phone and dialled his favourite cab driver. *He will be there in about 10 minutes*, the cab driver said. Ten minutes sounded like an hour!

When He finally arrived at the client's house, he found Melinda already packed and waiting by the elevator. Ignoring the pleasantries, she rushed through the usual instructions by him: the client had his bath, got dressed and is ready for breakfast. Khaya tried to explain his lateness, but Melinda wouldn't listen. She stepped right into the elevator with the door closing almost immediately. Khaya let himself in to the client's apartment with his key.

Caregiving was not always about the challenges and hazards of the job. Yes, there was the usual stress associated with the job, the exhaustion, anxieties about clients falling and hurting themselves, as well making sure you don't get infected with some horrible disease as a caregiver. Caregiving was also about the fun things. The joy derived from helping clients do what they love doing. The short walks with the clients, the games, and the part where you get to watch their favourite movies, sports or shows with them—Khaya even picked up new sporting interests in the process.

Some clients are VIPs in their own right. Others have rubbed shoulders with VIPs and would beam with pride, as they share their memories and memorabilia with the caregiver. It wasn't unusual for caregivers to accompany their clients to special events, exclusive dinners, parties, and Operas. Even a ride in an EMT vehicle as surreal as it were, could leave the caregiver feeling like being a part of a medical soap opera.

Even though the caregiver may have started out merely for the money and survival, most caregivers eventually fall in love with their job, and become emotionally attached to the clients. Clients and carers forming a special bond, they sometimes become inseparable.

It is just the nature of the job.

The new client was in her late seventies.

She was unmarried and had no children but had a sister in Chicago. She lived in a luxurious facility for seniors in downtown Orlando. Khaya figured she must have earned a lot of money in her working years or inherited a lot of it. The facility was one of the highly prized homes in the city.

She stayed in the independent wing of the facility—the section for seniors who needed minimal care—often called, *Independent Living*. The other wing was for seniors who required 24-hour assistance. This wing was referred to as, *Assisted Living*. The entire facility was well-equipped with recreational areas, a large dining room and common area or TV room. There was also a state-of-the-art gym and a medical room. Many of the luxury apartments had balconies facing the beautiful courtyard. It was simply for the rich.

Khaya's client had extremely bad dementia. She slept for most of the day and never wanted to get out of her chair. His job was to get her to respond to him, to ensure that she baths, got dressed and go about her morning routine—which included joining her friends for meals in the dining area, play board games, going for a walk and sometimes doing light stretches. However, it was always a struggle to get her to do any of it. She would stay in bed all day with the windows cracked open, even in the dead of winter, leaving Khaya to freeze.

Her couch was her safe haven. On Khaya's first day, she had asked for a leg massage as she laid on the couch. Khaya didn't see anything obnoxious about that. Clients often asked for feet massages. However, in her case, the massages extended far longer than normal. She would resist if he tried to stop–continuously asking for more and making weird annoying sounds. It was one of those rare moments that Khaya would snap at a client. She would get really upset and pout until he left.

Because of her dementia, the same scenario would play out the next day, every day. Khaya reported to Kegan who promised to speak with the client. He doubted he ever did. Even though it was unethical to share information about a client with a third party, Khaya couldn't help but share with Bayo the strange request from the client. He found it funny but not surprised. He had encountered similar oddities during his time as a caregiver as well.

Everything changed when Melinda told him about the client's secret crush. She would only leave the room to play board games with a male resident. She would even decline to play with any other person, if this senior wasn't in the room, such was the extent of her infatuation with this man. Khaya knew he had stumbled on gold.

He colluded with his counterpart, the man's caregiver to arrange regular meal and game times. It was quite unbelievable, maybe not actually, to see the excitement on her face whenever she heard that her 'crush' was going to be in the dining room, or in the game room. It made their lives a lot easier. Catching feelings it seems, has no bounds.

Much like the rest of the human organs, age plays a major part in recovery from a heart ache. When an eighty-year-old's heart gets hurt, the pain is beyond description. It was the case when the elderly bloke appeared for dinner one evening, dressed in a lovely, tailored suit and a bow tie, with a lady in tow, immaculately dressed in an evening gown. They both looked dashing, almost like young couples out on a date. Khaya's client was devastated. She was more upset because of the chosen woman. Apparently, there had been some squabbles between the two ladies before Khaya's time.

Without warning, his client rushed up from her chair, and stormed out of the dining room, leaving Khaya chasing after her. It was ridiculous. *These are grandparents for crying out loud*, he thought to himself.

That evening, she demanded an even longer leg massage. He had never been happier to see Melinda arrive for the night shift!

The next day, she asked Khaya to hurry up. She didn't want to miss the board game with her crush. Khaya was astounded, but then he remembered...

He continued to juggle both shifts to the detriment of his academic work.

Khaya was behind in his schoolwork. He missed several deadlines. He spoke with Kegan about taking a few days off his schedule during the week, in order to attend to some urgent schoolwork. He also arranged with a friend on campus to stay with him for the week, all in a bid to catch up on lost academic time.

His program advisor was not sympathetic. He wanted to know why he was behind in his work, and risking losing his funding. He reminded him of his scholarship conditions–which Khaya had completely forgotten about. He realised he could truly lose his funding except he managed to achieve a significant turnaround in his results. He had to achieve a minimum of 3.67 GPA in his overall grade at the end of the academic year. By all indications, it looked like a tall order. But he was used to climbing mountains.

He called Kegan to update him on his challenges. They agreed to cut down his hours. He could keep the Smiths, but only for two eight-hour shifts in the week.

It was the month of May.

Nelson Mandela was being inaugurated as the first

black president of South Africa.

Bayo and Khaya remained glued to the TV all day. It was an incredible moment of history unfolding in their very eyes. Khaya had been making calls all day. His parents had also called to keep him up to date with events in the country. They had told him about the week long parades on the streets of Cape Town. They wanted to know what the feeling was like in the States, *were they also celebrating?* They asked. All the Cable TVs had been covering the build up to the inauguration, with clips of Mandela's 1990 visit to the white house playing on air intermittently. The world was agog. A promise fulfilled, a dream come true. South Africa was the darling of the world.

Presidents and international celebrities jostled for seats at the most televised event of the last few decades—since Princess Diana's wedding.

He missed home but he had work to do.

Mr Smith was a little sluggish. It took longer to get him ready. Hungry and tired, Khaya went to the kitchen to pick up his breakfast. Mrs Smith was busy making some milk tarts and cakes. She offered him some. He thanked her and picked up two cupcakes from the tray.

He joined the client in the living room to watch a

heated political debate being broadcast on TV. It was a critical election year for both the Democrats and the Republicans. Bill Clinton was in the middle of his presidency and there were strong indications that the Republicans might win back, majority of the seats in the US House, something not seen since the 50's. Mr Smith was convinced the Democrats would retain House majority. Khaya could never understand American politics. Even his client had fallen asleep in the middle of the debate.

As he got up to take his plates to the kitchen, he heard Simone in the kitchen with her mother. He didn't realise she was coming to visit. Usually the dad would have mentioned it out of excitement, and would want to be all ready and dressed up on time. *It must be a surprise visit*, Khaya thought, as he joined the ladies in the kitchen.

Surprisingly, she was warm towards him. She asked about his family, and wanted to know if he had plans to go home to join in the celebration of the new president. She told him she would love to visit South Africa. He learnt she was in Kenya during her college years. Khaya finished doing his dishes, and excused himself to check on her dad.

The next morning, Simone asked if he had been around the property yet. He told her he hadn't had the time to do so. He had been working on his term paper in his free time. She promised to take him on a tour of the property before she left for New York. Khaya became suspicious of the sudden attention she was giving him.

Later that day, Khaya sat outside on the porch to work on his paper. He had just settled the client into his recliner for his afternoon nap. Khaya had worked on his paper all night, and was hoping he could submit before the end of the day, once he was done with the referencing. The lecturer had been kind to grant him an extension.

He was engrossed in his work, when he suddenly had the feeling that someone was watching him. Khaya turned around and there she was, the client's daughter. She quickly apologised for sneaking up on him, and confessed that she had been reading parts of his paper. He was irritated. He told her it was impolite to sneak up on people.

She walked over and sat next to him. Ignoring his comment on politeness, she asked what the paper was about. He told her that it was a term paper that was already due for submission. He was hoping she'd get the message and let him be.

Simone was relentless. She was bent on having small talks. It infuriated him further that she thought she could just interrupt him with no care in the universe. Frustrated, Khaya closed his laptop, and attempted to get up. She stopped him.

She asked if he was taking a break from his work, and if he would like to do the tour. He wasn't interested, all he wanted was to finish his paper and send it in. But he had a feeling she wasn't going to take no for an answer. She was demanding that he give her his time. He knew she was thinking, *it was paid for anyway*.

Khaya tried another excuse. He told her he wasn't sure her mother would approve of him leaving the client to go on a tour of the property. She told him not to worry about her mum. She went inside the house. He could see her talking to her mum in the living room. When she returned, she told him her mum was okay with it. The dad was still enjoying his nap. *They'd be back in a minute*, she said.

There was no doubt that the house was magnificent. The interior of the house had a baronial touch to it. Beautiful and homely, it was befitting for royalty. But when Simone took him further into the grounds, his heart stopped.

They descended the flight of stairs, and walked around the side of the house, leading to an even bigger expanse of land, with the most impressive landscaping of all time. He was dumbfounded. There was an array of beautifully planted flowering shrubs, that spread across the grounds. Lining the well-sculptured pathway, were some of the most exotic hydrangeas, azaleas and camellias he's ever seen. It was every horticulturist's dream! His nasal senses led him towards another bunch of plants in the distance, close to a tall gazebo–with a space the size of an average living room. It was the Brunfelsia Pauciflora plant, with its array of beautiful flowers, of all kinds of colours imaginable–shades of dark blue, lilac and white.

It brought him a feeling of nostalgia. The Brunfelsia Pauciflora plant, also called, *'Yesterday-Today-And-Tomorrow'*, were one of his favourites back home. His parents had inherited the plants from their parents, who had imported the seeds from Germany in the early 1900's. The leaves are leathery with some sort of shiny sheen to them. The flowers, leave the garden with a distinctively sweet scent.

It was surreal to see those plants. Khaya drifted away from her. He walked to the plants, almost caressing its beautiful flowers. He suddenly felt very homesick. Simone came up to him and asked if he liked the plants. He smiled, and told her that they had similar plants back home. He had grown up playing maze with those plants. He learnt everything he knew about plants from their gardener, who was also Mammi's boyfriend, he told her.

Simone was curious. She wanted to know which happened first, being the boyfriend or being the gardener, how they got married and if the gardener is now his step-father? Khaya laughed. Careful not to give away too much, "No, they never got married," he replied.

Khaya and Simone sat for a while in the huge gazebo. She repeated the story about her trip to Kenya. It was as an exchange program her school offered during her final years at the university. It was still one of her best moments, she had said, even though she had returned home sick to death from malaria. She still looked forward to returning to Africa again sometime in the future.

"Have you travelled the continent?" she asked. He remained measured in his responses. He was uncomfortable with the openness with which the Americans spoke. *They had no restraints,* he thought. He was still trying to get used to the culture. Khaya volunteered some of his Pan-African convictions. He would also like to travel the length and breadth of the continent. He had read of so many historic and powerful societies in the continent.

They sat in silence for a while, each savouring the beautiful scenery. It actually felt good being out. "Would it be okay to bring your father out here every now and then?" Khaya asked her. "Of course," she replied. He would love to. She told him how she loved running around the grounds with him as a child, playing golf and sometimes baseball. She was the son he secretly wished he had. Her father loved nature, and would spend his mornings out in the garden every day before work. *Yes, he would love the walk in the garden*, she repeated, as she got up to show him the remaining part of the property.

They stood on a gigantic rock formation. It was her favourite spot on the property, she told him. The rocks were assembled about twenty years ago. It had the most spectacular view of the property from the top of the rocks. He could see a large stream of water, a river running through the grounds and into oblivion. She said it flowed from the surrounding lake, a landmark of Winter Park. The flowing river had such a calming effect—he could just sit there staring into the river for eternity.

The tour came to an abrupt end once they realised how much time had gone past. She needed to get ready for a business meeting in town that evening, and was sure her dad was already up, and wondering where his favourite caregiver was.

They walked back to the house, each lost in thoughts. Mrs Smith met them at the door as they came in. She had a curious look on her face. Khaya side-stepped her, and quickly made his way to the client. He was up and watching the news channel. He asked if he enjoyed the walk with his daughter. Embarrassed, Khaya responded that they had a beautiful house. "Are you ready for dinner?" he asked, changing the subject quickly.

The whole encounter left him feeling awkward.

He did everything he could to avoid her. He was glad when she left for New York the following day, or was he really?

He made a mistake telling Bayo about the tour. He wanted to know every detail. What did they talk about? How was her demeanour? The more he tried to end the conversation, the more Bayo wanted to know. He thrived in making mountains out of molehills.

Simone was different from her mother. She had her father's piercing eyes, the type that makes you jittery. She had an uncanny beauty, and her mother's strong personality. She had studied law like her father, and worked as an attorney with one of the top law firms in New York.

Her parents were distraught when she moved north. Her father wanted her to join his legal practice, but she had other plans. She had always wanted to step out of her parent's shadows. Her mother had taken over the forestry and logging business from her father, and grown it into a multinational business with presence in Europe and Asia, while her father had concentrated on growing his law firm.

Ever since she was a child, she had always felt pressured, albeit a subtle one. She was an only child. Her parents had struggled to conceive immediately after their wedding. Simone was born twelve years into their marriage. She came into their world with her life plan surgically attached to her chest, one meticulously drawn up by her parents in their twelve years of waiting.

She would spend the rest of her life trying to redraw the plan.

Her plan didn't include marriage. Her parents thought at twenty-nine, she should be taking the matter more seriously. She reminded them over and over that her immediate goal was to make partner at her firm. She didn't think there was room for marriage yet. In any case, her boyfriend didn't seem to care about any such commitments. He was happy the way things were, and just like her, was not ready for marriage or children, she had explained to them. Her mother could never understand her ways. *What is a woman without a home of her own?* She would often ask.

Life continued as normal at the Smiths.

It had been over six weeks since he saw her. Khaya had been taking her father for occasional walks in the garden. He was also spending more of his free time on the rock formation, remembering the moment they shared together listening to the sound of the river flowing.

He had denied it when Bayo alleged that he was missing her. Maybe he was, but what was there to miss? As far as he knew, that was just one moment that wouldn't happen again. *She was usually rude and dismissive, not a trait to miss*, Khaya reminded himself.

In a moment of poor judgement, Khaya had asked about her from the dad. He thought it was unlike her to not visit for that long. The father smiled. He told him she was fine. She was busy with a high-profile case, "I'll be sure to let her know you asked," he quipped.

They were in the garden some days later, when the client broke the news to him. Simone would be visiting with her boyfriend the next day. It would be the first time they would be meeting him, and they weren't sure what to expect. He joked that the daughter always took off her smart hat when it came to picking men.

Khaya was relieved. He was sure that would put an end to the silly insinuations from Bayo. He was right. She was only trying to get him to loosen his guards by pretending to be nice and friendly.

Simone arrived the next day as planned. She walked straight to her father's room. Khaya had just finished helping him into his walker when she barged in. She took a cursory glance at him, said hello, and threw her arms around her father. He kissed her, and asked where the boyfriend was, and if he got a cold feet or changed his mind. She laughed. "He is with mum," she said, as she guided him out of the room.

Khaya remained in the room, unsure if he was expected to join them or not. He joined anyway. His place was with his client always, the trainer had told them during his orientation.

Everyone turned to him as he entered the room. Their eyes met. He could tell she was puzzled. He recovered quickly, made the connection, and proceeded to introduce himself. Khaya took the outstretched hand, and before he could say anything, Simone chipped in, "Khaya is my dad's caregiver. He is South African and also studying for his bachelor's at UF." "Is that right?" the boyfriend responded with an air of arrogance. "How's Mandela?" he added. Khaya didn't respond. Khaya always assumed people meant it as a rhetorical question and thus never bothered to respond.

Later at dinner, he got to know more about the boyfriend. They had met at a conference in Detroit earlier in the year. *And we fell in love so fast, we couldn't wait to get married*, Khaya whispered to himself mischievously. She decided to join him, and had asked him over to her parent's house when she realised he'd be in Florida for the week on business.

Mrs Smith smiled approvingly at her daughter. Khaya was sure she was already imagining wedding bells.

"What do you think of him?" The client asked him as he prepared him for bed. Khaya wasn't sure how to respond. So he asked what he meant. The client asked what he thought of Simone's boyfriend. He hesitated for a moment. He had thought the boyfriend was okay. He was quite conversational and seemed to really like Simone. "He seemed like a good person," Khaya responded. The client nodded, reached for the TV remote, and tuned to the Late Night Show.

Just as Khaya was about to sit, he heard the client whisper aloud, "Yeah, but he never could stop talking." Khaya chuckled, but said nothing. He watched the remote drop to the bed, tucked the client in properly and he left for his room. It had been a very long day. He was sure the two love birds were out partying for the rest of the evening.

She rested her head on his lap.

The quietness disturbed by the sound of the flowing river. He rubbed his fingers through her hair. It didn't feel right but it also felt good. She was his client's daughter.

Bayo had been right all along. He should listen to him more.

Simone raised her head to his. He looked into her eyes again as he kissed her. "I love you," Khaya whispered, just as a familiar sound rang through from the distance. It was his phone alarm. Khaya jumped out of bed in an instant. He rushed out of the room to the client. He had overslept. He only had a few minutes to prepare the client before the next caregiver arrives.

He was even more rattled by the dream.

Khaya's mind drifted home.

It had been over a year since he left home, since the murders. Yet, the police hadn't made any breakthrough in their investigations, in spite of their claim of finding a strong lead.

The police had been trying to solve the mystery behind the neighbours' claim that they had not heard any dog barks preceding the sound of the gun shots. The police thought they knew why the dog hadn't barked before it was poisoned. But that was some months ago. It didn't seem like they were making any headway.

It was frustrating to think that Mammi and Leanne's killers were still out there, at large. The investigating officer was now avoiding his calls. He had resisted calling his parents. He was sure the last thing they wanted was him calling to add to their frustrations.

He looked out of the bus window, still lost in thoughts.

His mind drifted again. He remembered the dream. It felt so real. *What business was it of his to dream about her like that?*, he thought to himself.

And suddenly, he felt a soft touch on his shoulder. It was not his thoughts. Khaya turned around and saw a woman of African descent and with dreadlocked hair that covered her entire face—he could only see her eyes. She leaned towards him from the seat behind.

She sat alone. She spoke in an accent that was difficult to place, it had a melodious ring to it, different from what he'd heard from other Africans.

"What is the problem, my child?" She asked almost in a whisper. "Excuse me?" Khaya blurted out, shocked and lost for words."I see a dark cloud hovering around you. It is a bad omen my child. Your 'Ori' is troubled," the strange woman continued unperturbed. "What have you done?" Khaya was dumbstruck.

He had seen many mentally ill people on the streets. He had also encountered some at bus stations and on buses. He never thought much of them, beyond mere drug addicts or just destitute. But none had gone to this extent.

Khaya turned away from the woman, completely disgusted. He almost fell off his chair when she added, "you have left your home in disarray, it needs you." Khaya turned around again, but this time, the strange women got up abruptly, pressed the emergency bus stop, and dashed to the bus exit. Khaya stared at her, now shaken. She shot him another look as she disembarked and disappeared into the morning chill.

———

"Oh my gosh!" Khaya screamed into the open

laptop computer.

Alarmed, Bayo rushed to see what the excitement about. "What's up?" he asked, trying to catch a glimpse of the text on the screen. Khaya could only point to the open message in his inbox. Bayo leaned in. The email subject read "Re: Cancellation of Study Grant. Exasperated, he slumped to the floor, and laid on the carpet with his head facing the ceiling. *What is going on?* he moaned, as a million thoughts running through his mind. Bayo was equally distraught. He wanted him to ask for a review. *There was no way that could be the final verdict, could it?* He asked rhetorically.

And then Khaya remembered the weird woman on the bus earlier that day.

He sat up. "You know it's strange," Khaya started. The weirdest thing happened today, on the bus home. He went on to narrate the story of the woman on the bus, and how she had mentioned something about him running away from home, and something about an 'Ori'.

Bayo interjected. "Did she say 'Ori'?" he asked. This woman, could she be Nigerian? Khaya said he couldn't say for sure. She could be from anywhere. But 'Ori' was a spiritual construct of the Yoruba people, an Ethnic group in Nigeria.

Bayo had heard many stories back home of people encountering strangers in all sorts of places, who spoke about matters known only to the individual being addressed, and in some cases not known to any man or woman. He was conversant with the concept of 'Ori'. He had seen many local movies, and read many books including articles, alluding to its primacy.

'Ori', which also means "head" in Yoruba culture, can be linked to the concept of 'destiny'. A form of human consciousness—spiritual and physical—that's infused into our essence as humans. This human consciousness is often worshipped as a divinity, called 'Orisha'. The Yorubas' believe that humans can take control of their destinies by worshipping the 'Orishas', in order to achieve success in life.

It is believed that when things are not going right, one should consult his or her 'Ori', and make sacrifices, a kind of appeasement to the 'Orishas', in order to turn things around for the better. Bayo was sure similar beliefs existed in other African cultures.

Khaya had never heard of it. He dismissed it as merely a fable—even as he struggled to shake off the feeling from his encounter with the weird woman on the bus. He joked that Bayo, a scientist, should know better than to try to reverse Western civilisation. Bayo disagreed. He countered that it was the 'whiteness' in Khaya speaking. "No, it's the enlightenment in me, you mean?" Khaya fought back, as the sparring continued. Bayo didn't see anything enlightened about dismissing one's culture or traditions. He should wake up, Bayo added.

Khaya was infuriated. He had spent his childhood defending his blackness. Who was he to tell him about culture and heritage? What did he know about identity crisis, and the challenges people face daily, simply because of circumstances of their birth? Khaya was livid. "It's not like you go around wearing a *dashiki* and animal hides yourself," he retorted sarcastically, as he stormed out of the room.

Khaya called the office of the funding coordinator the next day. He wanted to know what the procedure was for appealing a cancellation of grant. The coordinator asked him to send an email with his request. It was already close of business in South Africa when he called. Khaya sent an email accordingly.

He asked for a reversal given how much work he had put in during the last quarter, as evident in his grades. He also visited his program advisor at the university. There has to be something the school could do to assist him. Maybe they could send a letter of support in his benefit to the Foundation.

On a busy October morning, Khaya received two separate voice messages on his phone. One was from his father. He wanted him to return his call as soon as possible. It was about the police investigation. The second message was from the investigating officer himself. They may have had a breakthrough in the investigation. He also wanted him to call as soon as he could.

Khaya was elated. He looked at his watch. It was a good time to call. He dialed the officer.

They had arrested one of the perpetrators. Khaya wanted to know if they had a confession. The officer didn't want to give out much information. He told him that they had also updated his parents. They expect to bring the suspect to court in a matter of weeks.

Khaya called his dad. He confirmed what he had always suspected, but feared to say aloud. The police had arrested Khwezi, Mammi's former boyfriend and their former gardener. Khaya had told himself it was improbable that Khwezi could be involved in such a gruesome crime. Yes, their relationship had ended bitterly. But he only had himself to blame for it—with the drugs and alcohol abuse— it was bound to end one way or another. Khaya was glad when Mammi had ended it before it was too late, or so he had thought.

But he was also a kind-hearted man, when he was not under the influence. He had been very nice to him as a child. He was patient with him whenever he ran across the garden while he worked. He taught him everything he knew about gardening.

His dad went on to tell him that the police had followed a lead to Swaziland where Khwezi had fled to all these years. He had confessed to the identity of his co-conspirator, whom the police found had been killed in a cash heist some months back. The case would be going to court in a matter of days. His dad and mum planned to attend the court sessions.

Khaya wasn't in support of that. He thought it would be traumatic for them. He asked to speak with his mother. The rift between them seemed to have been healed by the news of the arrest. She was overjoyed that the criminals had been arrested. She was riled that someone she had opened her home to, had turned around to inflict irreparable damage on her family. She wanted to know if Khaya would be home for the trial. South Africa was also opening up now, she added. "Finish up quickly, and come back home. The new government is kicking out the whites and replacing them with blacks, even those with little education," she added characteristically.

Khaya waited impatiently for response from the Black Excellence Foundation. It's been four weeks since he sent his appeal application. His program officer had also come through for him. He provided an excellent support letter attesting to the significant improvements in his grades towards the later part of his studies, a proof that if given the chance, Khaya could improve his overall grades to meet the required level.

It was important that they reinstate his funding. He barely survived on his wages from his part-time work. There was no way he could afford the twenty thousand dollar annual tuition.

He thought of calling his dad, to put him on notice. After all, he had asked about his studies and again offered to help in any way if he needed him. He would wait to hear from the scholarship committee. Who knows, maybe his client may volunteer to write him a cheque, now how about that for a real dream. He reveled in his power of imagination.

Khaya arrived early for his shift, and so did Christmas.

It was the middle of November. The garden, as well as the interior of the house, had been beautifully decorated. Christmas lights adorned every available space. It was indeed a spectacle—some called it a capitalist gimmick. Khaya always loved the feeling of Christmas since he was a child. It had the good effect of transporting one into the fantasy world of Santa Claus! In his opinion, it does the world more good than harm.

Simone was home. She had arrived the week before.

She was in the living room as he entered the house. It was the first time they'd be alone together since their tour.

They chatted for a while. He was tempted to ask her about her boyfriend but thought against it. Instead, he let her do most of the talking. She wanted to know if he had any plans for the holiday, if he'd be travelling back home. Khaya told her he didn't have any plans yet, and was certainly not travelling.

She invited him to join them for Christmas. He suddenly remembered he had promised to join Bayo and some other friends for a Christmas party in Houston. There was no way he'd sit around with the client's family for Christmas. Thanks, but no, he wouldn't be able to. He told her. She quipped that she was sure there was a woman waiting. She wouldn't want an angry woman storming their house. He bit his tongue, and excused himself to go check on his client.

Khaya observed that the client had been unusually unresponsive. He seemed lethargic. Khaya quickly did the vitals. His blood pressure was extremely high. He rushed to notify his daughter.

She asked if the previous caregiver had noticed anything. Khaya wasn't sure. If she had, she sure didn't tell him. He sent a quick message to his colleague to ask if she had noticed anything unusual about the client the night before.

The wife also joined them in the room, as soon as came in and held his face, she immediately asked Khaya to call the emergency line. He had to be taken to the hospital immediately, she ordered.

The EMT arrived swiftly. Khaya rode with him to the hospital while the wife and daughter called the family doctor to notify him. They locked up, and drove to the hospital.

Khaya wished he had gone straight to the client as soon as he had arrived at the house—maybe he could have saved him from the stroke. The doctor thought he had been lucky. If he had not been attended to immediately, he may have suffered a severe brain damage.

He remained in the ICU while they conducted a series of brain scans to determine the extent of the damage. He was a high-risk patient, given his existing conditions and age. The doctor warned that it was particularly difficult for stroke patients who are elderly to make a full recovery, but he remained hopeful, and wanted the family to be as well. They were all devastated. Khaya excused the wife and daughter as they both burst into tears upon hearing the diagnosis.

Khaya stayed with the client at the hospital. Mrs Smith asked her daughter if she could take him to get his bag. Khaya had never seen her so vulnerable.

They drove in silence for the first mile. Each burdened by the reality of what just happened. He broke the silence. It was the first time since his own loss that he spoke about his feelings. He had not been able to talk about it with anyone. It just hurt so much. But for some reason, it felt right to talk to her. To share her fears and her pain in the moment.

He told her he understood what she was going through. The fear of losing a loved one is probably more crippling than actually losing them. He told her how he had stayed day and night by Mammi's bed, as she went through several surgeries to try and save her from the fatal gunshot, but she never woke up. He went on to explain how he had been unable to look at the lifeless body of Leanne, his sister, who had died on the scene. He told her how their family had become broken by guilt, that they each carried subsequent to the tragedy. He was sure his mother blamed his dad for bringing the 'black family' into their lives.

He told her how he was adopted as a child, and how he later rebelled against everything that he knew growing up: his family, his friends and even himself. By the time he realised how much pain he was inflicting on those who loved him, through his act of selfishness, it was too late. He wished he had another chance to tell his sister and Mammi how sorry he was, and how much he loved them.

Simone was sorry. She had no idea he carried so much pain. She told him she was sure his sister and Mammi are now angels, and they can see his pain. She reminded him that he had an opportunity to make it up to his parents. She would make sure she let hers know how much she loved them too.

When they arrived at the house, Khaya thanked her for the ride and apologised for his soppiness. He also thanked her for not killing him with her crazy driving. She laughed and told him she was glad he enjoyed her driving.

Khaya excused himself. He wanted to have a quick shower—after the ride in the EMT and all—and get ready to go back to the hospital to relieve her mum. He also wanted to quickly get away from her—the ride had again made him feel a little uncomfortable.

He couldn't get rid of the knots in his stomach.

He had just stepped into the shower when he thought he heard the bathroom door creak open. As he swung around, his heart leapt...

She stood at the door, her eyes fixed on him. Instinctively, khaya covered his privates with his hands, as he crouched towards the towel rack. But she was faster. She grabbed the towel, and dangled it teasingly. He let his hands free, as he watched her reveal the most beautiful body he had ever seen.

The last thing he heard was something about her hair, and it was back to dreamland.

Mrs Smith asked why Simone hadn't came back to the hospital. He mumbled something about her getting some groceries. The mother wanted to leave, but wanted a family member there with the dad. Khaya suspected it might be her hair appointment. She called her daughter to find out if she was coming. She told her she'd be there in an hour. Simone explained that she had to quickly drop off some items at the father's office. He hoped she didn't give much thought to his crossed wires.

Alone with the client, Khaya recalled the events of the last hour, with a grin on his face.

They had ended up on the couch in the living room.

Khaya wriggled out of her embrace and reminded her that they were expected back at the hospital. Her mum would be waiting.

He dashed to his room. Got dressed, packed his laptop and grabbed some snacks from the kitchen. She was still on the couch when he returned. She told him to go ahead. She would need some more time to get ready, and dry her hair. She would join them later, she said. He called a meter cab.

Simone arrived few hours later. Her mother dashed out immediately and told Khaya to please call her if there was an emergency. He was glad that they were not alone in the room. The attending nurse was around most of the time, taking vitals and replacing the intravenous fluids.

He never could understand how she did it. She always appeared composed, while he shook like a leaf in the aftermath of both encounters.

Maybe he read too much into these things, or maybe it was just an act. But it sure felt like she was used to having men like him at will. The way she had acted. It was the hallmark of someone who knew how to get what she wanted. His feeling of Eldorado quickly gave way to embarrassment.

He would wait for a moment alone with her to ask if *they were ok*. He hoped it wouldn't mean the end of his job. He couldn't afford to lose his job now. He had applied to another agency for an extra shift— he didn't think Kegan would be keen to reinstate his other shift after the school drama, but they were yet to get back to him.

Maybe he should just have asked her to leave the moment he saw her in his bathroom, or maybe he should have fled instead. How stupid can he be? Khaya scolded himself, as he prepared to stay the night with the client. Simone had left a little earlier. He promised to call her if anything happened.

Khaya couldn't sleep. He worked on his laptop most of the night, while also keeping watch over his client. He was still nervous about the outcome of his funding review. The board had promised to give him feedback in the coming days.

On the morning of his last shift, he sent a message to the other caregiver to update her on the client's progress. The doctors were happy with the client's progress. He seemed to have stabilised. The client would be moved to outpatient care in matter of days. She would report straight to the hospital to relieve him.

Later that evening as he got ready to leave, the mother again suggested that Simone drop him off. He was about to scream, 'No', when he heard her agree to her mum's request. Khaya tried to resist.

He told them it was no trouble getting a cab. Mrs Smith would have nothing of it. He bade goodbye to the client and his colleague, as he walked out of the room with Simone to his side. She was on the phone with her boyfriend halfway into the drive. He felt uncomfortable listening to their conversation on the car's audio system. He tried to occupy himself with his phone, but couldn't help listening in. Her boyfriend was going to be in Miami in two days and would try to fly up to them. He was sorry about her dad and wished him soonest recovery. She told him she missed him, and ended the call. She apologised for the call—even though Khaya didn't know why she apologised—and asked if he wanted to get something for the road. Khaya resisted as he still had the sandwich her mum had given him at the hospital.

Khaya inhaled slowly, and asked about her boyfriend. As expected, she was dismissive. She told him they weren't that serious. She told him she was sure she'd end up single, which wouldn't be bad, she added. She thought relationships were too complicated, and she is too old for such games. Khaya laughed so hard, Simone had to ask if it was what she said. He apologised, and told her it was just funny that she, barely thirty-years-old, would think herself too old for matters of the heart. A former client of his, well over seventy, flirted with an eighty-year-old man, and had her heart ripped out. When he told her how his client would dress up every day hoping to see him at dinner, and how on the fateful night, he had showed up with another damsel in red, she cracked up so much.

One way or another, she ended up driving him to the house. She promised she'd be quick. She just had to pick up some essentials and would drop him off at the bus station. He could stay in the car if he wanted. She suddenly returned to the car. She had thought the house cleaner was in, but only remembered she was running errands for her, as she got to the door. She came to the car to retrieve her house keys. She asked if he was sure he didn't want to come inside. There was something about the way she asked. Khaya mulled the thought. He stepped out of the car few minutes later.

As he walked into the living room, he saw her standing by one of the family portraits. It was the picture of them in Europe. She told him they had gone skiing at the Austrian Alps that winter.

Khaya moved closer to her. She leaned into him as he wrapped his hands around her. "Oh, that feels good", she moaned softly. He held in tighter just as she turned around to face him, their eyes locked. He bent slightly to kiss her. He could feel her longing. "What about the housekeeper?" Khaya asked. She responded with more kisses, as she led him to the couch.

The housekeeper returned just as they were driving off. "Phew! That was close," she said, as they both burst into laughter.

———

Hamba uye ekhaya! Hamba uye ekhaya! (You have to go home, you have to go home), Mammi cried out.

"Mammi! Mammi!" Khaya shouted. But she disappeared before he could reach her.

Bayo rushed to Khaya's room. He had been up watching late night soccer when he heard him scream aloud. The screams were become rampant.

Khaya had been having similar dreams in recent days. She was always upset with him in the dreams, and instructing him to go home. He would often wake up from the dreams, sad and confused. It was as if she was trying to tell him something.

Everything seemed to be happening at once. The dreams as well as the encounter with the strange woman on the bus. His mind was in turmoil, he told Bayo.

"Maybe we should try seeking out answers," Bayo told him. "Answers? How and where?" Khaya wanted to know. He had no idea what to do or where to go with all the things happening to him. The only person that could possibly help was his aunt, and he hadn't spoken to her in ages.

Bayo knew of a Nigerian church downtown. He had only attended the church twice, but some of his friends were regular members of the church. They often bragged about their new pastor who had just been deployed from home. If he didn't mind a little drama, he could take him there to meet with the pastor, Bayo told him. He warned him that it was somewhat different from the 'regular churches'.

Khaya and Bayo had attended a Pentecostal church nearby, and he liked it. It was similar to the one back home where the family attended—not that they were a particularly religious family, at least not him, but they were not unbelievers either. He enjoyed the church service the few times he attended, but had tried not to get too involved. He always made sure to excuse himself immediately after service.

The following Sunday, he went with Bayo to the 'Nigerian church'. It was every bit the spectacle

Bayo had described, and more.

He had seen videos of African churches back at home, with bogus claims of spiritual powers and healings. He had also seen images of traditional healers in Mammi's apartment. She had called them 'Sangomas', people with divine powers to heal others of all sorts of spiritual sickness. But this was the first he'd be attending such a gathering. If this was where all the mysteries would be unravelled, then so be it. He was open to answers.

It was a very vibrant and colourful gathering of mostly Nigerians—with a handful of other Africans and African Americans. He spotted a white woman in the congregation, dressed in the popular and colourful Nigerian attire. Khaya guessed she must be connected to one of the Nigerian men in the church.

The choir was equally flamboyant. He enjoyed the music, or maybe the dancing more than the music. It was reminiscent of the charismatic African American choir. It was a soulful experience, he admmitted.

Everything about the church was extravagant, the sermon, prayers and all. Khaya was exhausted and couldn't stop thinking of his shift the next day. He still needed to pack his bags, so he can be ready for the first bus to work. But the sermon dragged on and on. He kept stealing glances at Bayo who just sat calmly and fixated on the pastor.

Eventually, the service ended. It had taken three hours.

Bayo led him to another section of the church building. It was the pastor's quarters. He told him they would be meeting with one of the church prophets. He explained that the prophets were specially gifted people, who had the gift of divination and were able to interpret dreams, and provide spiritual guidance. The prophets reported to the pastor, the head of church. Khaya was quite intrigued. If he thought the service was mind-blowing, the consultation with the prophet, would leave him completely bedazzled!

There were a number of people waiting in line to see the prophet. When it was their turn, Bayo introduced him to the prophet as his friend from South Africa.

"Hello, so you are from South Africa?" The prophet asked with a smile. "How's Mandela?" he added. As usual, Khaya let it slide.

The prophet went on to narrate stories about his visits to Durban and Cape Town, just a year after Mandela was released. He had been part of a contingent of church elders in Nigeria commissioned to meet with Mandela and Bishop Desmond Tutu, a renowned man of the cloth who was very vocal about his criticism of apartheid.

The prophet told him that South Africa was a blessed land. He believed that God had great plans for the people of South Africa, and just like the Israelites, the people of South Africa would overcome.

The prophet held his hand and dragged him to another end of the room. He asked him to kneel, and he immediately went into a trance-like mode, praying and singing at the same time. Khaya wasn't sure if he was meant to keep his eyes open or shut. He kept them open anyway, just in case.

The prayers ended abruptly as it begun. The prophet asked him to get up. He pulled two white plastic chairs closer and they both sat down.

The prophet started by asking if he knew how blessed he was? Khaya didn't respond.

The prophet continued, "I see you are a chosen and powerful one. The Lord has great plans for you." Khaya thought to himself that the prophet must be a fan of the phrase. The rest of the monologue— given Khaya had nothing to contribute—went the same way his dreams went. God wanted him to return home. His destiny is tied to his home, and no matter how long he stayed in the foreign land, he would still have to return home where he truly belongs. He shouldn't try resisting the call.

Khaya left the church feeling extremely exhausted.

He wasn't any closer to finding the answers he was hoping for. All the prophet had said at the end of the charade, was to be on the lookout for more signs. He told him he saw a vision of him leaving the country, but he wasn't sure to where. Khaya didn't have to tell him about his dreams anymore. He would have to continue seeking more answers, he thought to himself.

On their way home, Bayo asked if he wanted to reach out to his aunt. In his experience, sometimes when one has such incessant inclinations or dreams, it could be that something unpleasant had happened or about to happen to a loved one . It was not unusual in his culture, for someone to dream of loved ones who are in some distress of some sort. Perhaps he should check on his family, Bayo added.

Khaya was silent. What he hadn't mentioned to Bayo was that his mum had sent him a message earlier in the week. She wanted to inform him of his father's deteriorating health. He had been admitted recently for acute hypertension, but was now doing well. She didn't want him to be alarmed. He was in good hands, as he could imagine. She had said in her message.

Khaya had called his dad immediately. He was happy that he was doing well. He made a note to call him again that night as soon as they got home.

———

Her heart sank as she listened to the voice message her mum had left on her phone.

It had been a very busy day in court. Simone had been in Michigan representing a high-profile client. She had not had any free moment to check her phone.

When she switched it on, she was alarmed to find there were over 20 missed calls from her mother. And as she put the phone to her ears to listen to the voice message, she knew in that instant, that her life would never be the same again.

She finally managed to get her mother on the phone. She told him how they had found her dad slumped on the floor of their bedroom. The doctor's prognosis was a second stroke, a severe stroke that left him completely paralysed on both sides. She called Khaya. She was on the next available flight to Orlando she said.

The second stroke was brutal. He had slumped from his wheelchair while watching his favourite TV show. Khaya's colleague who had just returned from the bathroom, had immediately alerted the wife, and together they drove him to the hospital in the middle of the night.

It was barely a month after his first stroke. He had suffered severe brain damage. The doctor had told them that the prognosis wasn't good. They weren't sure if he'd survive the second attack. He was put on life support. They would keep him on life support for as long as they could, but he didn't think they should keep him on it for long. He would let the family decide.

Khaya joined the family at the hospital the following day. Simone and her mother were inconsolable. He left the room—it was too devastating to watch. He could feel all the emotions of his own personal loss rushing back.

Seeing seniors, in their end-of-life moments, can be both sad and inspiring. It often reminds one of the things that really matters in life. It is true that you get back what you give. This is even more important in cases of acute dementia, the love that's been sown and lives impacted, will rally round to make those last moments truly amazing. Caregivers observe with keen interest, those distinctions. They observe, through their clients last moments, lives that have been lived with impact, and ones lived in solitariness. The difference often manifests in the quality of care that the patients receives from their spouses, children, friends and family.

It is often a reflection of the depth of the built relationships. It matters not that the patient remembers or not, but the mere presence of family and friends during those moments speaks volume, at least for the observers.

It is heartening to watch grown up children sit around their ageing parents and give back years of love invested. However, it can also be heart-wrenching to see the opposite— where the children or spouse are visibly detached and can't wait for the end to come, or in some not too rare cases, seniors alone with their nurses or caregivers in their last moments.

Mr Smith was a very loving husband and father. He was loved by his friends and many in his community. Khaya had truly cared for him. He had a very intelligent and engaging mind—despite his medical condition. He was kind-hearted, and had a good sense of humour. It was very saddening to see him lay in bed helplessly, on a life support.

It was a difficult time for him and the family. It was also the end of his time with the family. Kegan had called to let him know that the client's family wouldn't need their services any longer.

Khaya said a prayer for Mr Smith, and wished his family well.

———————

The dreams were always the same.

There was always the old woman with a bunch of dripping wet leaves, rushing towards him. He always woke up just in time before she could get to him.

But this one was different...

He sat on a wooden rail, on the balcony of a dilapidated building, in what appeared to be a village. He was alone.Suddenly, he heard the sounds of a group of women chanting and dancing. The sound was coming from the center of the village.

Khaya got up from the railing, and followed the sound to the center of the village. As he approached, he saw three women. They were immaculately dressed in traditional Xhosa attires with impressive facial paintings. Engrossed in the beautiful chants of the women, he hadn't noticed another elderly woman beside him.

He felt someone nudge him. It was *Makhulu*, his grandmother. He was surprised to see her.

She placed her hand on his shoulder and told him that she was there with the rest of his ancestors.

In the same moment, she pointed towards the group of women dancing.

Mammi's image suddenly appeared. Her back was turned to him. He could see her dancing and chanting happily with the rest of the women. *Makhulu* told him that they had all come to celebrate his homecoming.

Confused, Khaya stepped away from her grip, and dashed towards Mammi. But the closer he got to the women, the further they were. He kept running, yelling and calling out her name, but they kept moving further away from him. Suddenly, there was silence. The dancing and chanting had stopped. Mammi walked away from the group. He could see her predisposition had changed. Khaya ran after her as she continued to walk away.

Then she turned around. He was terrified. Her eyes lit up in flames. It burned. He quickly turned away. She told him in an unmistakable voice, to go home, to his people. "Why Mammi? Who are my people?" Khaya cried out. But she had vanished. Everyone had. He searched frantically in the village for them, with tears streaming down his face, when suddenly he heard another voice.

The voice asked if he was okay. He opened his eyes. He was on the bus.

Khaya was embarrassed. He pressed the emergency stop—he would walk the rest of the journey home. He was shaken by the dream. It was the first time he was dreaming of her since her passing.

"I am sorry, Mama" he whispered, as he looked up to the heavens.

—————

It was the call that changed his destiny.

On a beautiful Wednesday morning, Khaya received a voice message from his program officer. He wanted him to call back urgently. They had received a response from his funders, he said. Khaya was taken aback. How come he hadn't received any notification? He wondered.

The program officer was sorry. His appeal had not been successful. His funding would not be reinstated. He would have to come up with alternative funding. The school would require a deposit from him within 14 days and an undertaking, on how he intends to settle the outstanding balance, in the absence of a credible sponsor. His program officer went on.

Khaya had not heard most of what he had said. He was deflated. He was also aware that failure to come up with the required payments would compel the university to report to the US Immigration and Customs Enforcement Agency (ICE), as required by the law. He could not believe what was happening to him.

He had hoped for some miracle. He could neither pay the seven thousand dollar deposit required in a few days, nor could he promise to pay the thirteen thousand dollars outstanding before the end of the session or forever for that matter.

He was only working one job and one shift since the Smith family cancelled their contract. There was no one he knew who could lend him such an amount either. His friend Bayo was merely living by on his middle class income. He always complained about how the middle in America is continually squeezed.

Khaya again thought about his dad. If he could borrow the money, maybe he could repay it if he worked even more shifts during holidays, but then there was still one more year left for his degree. He would still need to come up with the tuition for the final year. His dad was in poor health. It would be unfair to put such an additional burden on him. Besides, he would just have admitted total failure if he did that.

He put down his phone and went back to the client. The last thing he needed now was a senior falling and fracturing her hips under his watch.

He wondered if it had been worth it after all! Khaya received a call from Simone in late November of 1994.

She told him the family had decided to take the dad off life support. Khaya was speechless. He had known that day would come.

He wondered how she must be feeling.

"Are you ok?" he had asked, before realising how stupid he sounded. She was okay, she told him. She asked if he wanted to come say goodbye to him. They would all be gathered in his hospital room at 16:00 on the day. She added that his father was very fond of him. The family would want him there.

Mrs Smith and her daughter sat by the client's bed, while Khaya stood by the edge of the bed. The doctor had told them to talk to him as they would normally do. He was sure he could hear them. He rubbed his hands gently on the client's feet. It felt strange.

Khaya told him he still planned on taking him to South Africa as promised. It was difficult to remain composed. He thanked him for helping him find himself, fighting back the tears himself. When he looked at him lying on the bed, he saw Mammi as she laid in coma at the hospital.

Simone joked that he hoped her father wouldn't come back with a malaria infection, like she did when she went to Kenya. She asked if he remembered how he had flown to Oregon to be with her, as she prepared for her final exams in sick bed. How he had helped her with her Political Science and Criminal Law papers.

She kept stroking his hand with her head resting on his shoulder. She reminded him of how he had cooked for her and forced her to take the corn soup he made for her every day, even though he knew how much she hated it, but he insisted it was good for her. She promised him that she'd be fine, and would take care of mummy.

She told him that they knew he wanted to go.

The mother fought so hard to hide her tears, as she spoke of the first day she saw him in Idstein. How she prayed that he'd come up to her and say hello.

It was heartbreaking to watch.

Khaya thought of his adopted parents. All the love bestowed on him.

He knew in that moment that he needed to be with his family. His parents needed him now more than ever. There was nothing more fulfilling than caring for others, and letting those you love, know how much you really love them.

Khaya searched impatiently through his wardrobe.

He had no idea what to wear to the funeral. All he could find were a couple of jeans and shirts. He would look smarter in a suit, he though. Besides, everyone wore dark suits to funerals, didn't they? He asked Bayo if he could borrow one of his darker jackets—never mind the fit. He was sure he could get away with a little tightly fitted jacket. It wasn't like he was going to a dancing floor.

It was a private funeral. Khaya felt honoured, yet again, that he had been invited.

He went to Mrs Smith,sitted in the front row, where she sat with Simone, and registered his presence. He had already signed the funeral book placed at the church entrance.

Later that day, as he watched TV with Bayo, he heard his phone beep. It was a message from Simone. She wanted to know where he was. Khaya had quietly left the funeral service. He didn't want to hang around the family afterwards. He didn't think it was his place to do so. He told her he was home, watching TV. She sent another message. She wanted to come over.

Khaya thought she wanted him to come over, so he responded again, "I am sorry, it's a little late now," —he wasn't sure if he could get any busses now. He asked if it was okay if he came over the next day, assuming it wasn't urgent. She replied immediately, "No, no. I want to come over to your place." Khaya was stunned! This must be a prank, he thought, or maybe she was delusional. It must be the funeral, he reasoned.

She sent another message, 'What's the address? I am driving out now". Khaya showed the messages to Bayo. He was equally surprised. He asked if she had ever been to the house. "Of course not! Wouldn't you have known about that?" Khaya wanted to know what to do. "Just send the address", Bayo shouted. He couldn't understand his hesitation. I am sure she is only pulling your leg. Except, she wasn't. Simone arrived 30 minutes later. She asked that he buzz her in.

Khaya had to get rid of Bayo as soon as possible. He pleaded with Bayo to take a walk around the block for an hour or more. Bayo wanted 20 bucks for the favour, as long as she wasn't sleeping over, he said.

It had all been like a bad dream. She had thrown herself into the funeral planning, like a robot. She knew she had to be strong for her mother. The reality had hit her hard when she saw the casket lowered. It was hard to accept that her dad, her hero, was gone. She would never see him again. He would never smile back at her. She had been strong at the funeral, and hid her tears behind her sunglasses. But away from it all, and with him, she finally let it all out. She bawled, shaking in his warm embrace.

In that moment, she would forget the pain and sadness, as she cried out in pleasure, the type she had come to associate with him.

She wanted the moment to last forever.

Khaya looked at the time. It was already two hours since she arrived. Bayo would have completed a thousand laps around the block, he thought.

He wanted to know what she thought about him. He wasn't exactly sure how he felt,but he knew he really liked her. He had a feeling she didn't feel the same, but he'd like to know if he meant anything at all to her.

"So, how does it feel to be involved with two men at the same time?" Khaya asked, as she dressed up. She became irate, as she contined to get dress. "I don't know which men you are referring to," she retorted angrily. "As far as I am concerned, I am a single woman just having some fun."

It was the last time he would see her.

He felt so cheap! Yes, he wasn't suggesting that she was in love with him or something, but to throw the causality of it in his face, made him sick to his stomach. Just as well that he was no longer working with her family. It was a mistake from the very beginning, and not just the short lived rendezvous with her, but the whole idea that he could hide from his demons.

It seemed like he was stuck with them, whatever they were!

Simone left for New York a few days after the funeral.

She had tried to get her mother to come with her. She thought it might do her some good to take some time away and not be alone. But her mother, ever the independent one, declined her offer. She thought there was a lot to do between the logging company and the Law Firm. Dick would have wanted her to keep strong, she insisted.

Simone had thought about calling Khaya. She had felt a little guilty leaving the way she did. She thought she may have been a little insensitive. But she also didn't want to send the wrong message. She was not prepared for any more complications. It was bad enough that she was entangled in a relationship with a man she is desperately trying to get rid of—she didn't want to complicate matters by stringing another along.

If only she hadn't crossed he boundary the first time... or the second, but it was too late now. It was best to 'kill' it immediately, she thought to herself.

Thankfully, they didn't have to see each other again. She looked through her contacts, and without hesitation, deleted his phone number.

She hoped he would find the right woman, one that will make him happy. He was a good man.

Part Three

No Place like Home

It was a beautiful Saturday afternoon in Orlando.

Sunny with a cool wind.

Khaya sat on a wooden chair at a park, close to his apartment. A metal plate attached to the back of the chair caught his attention. The text showed that it was a donation in memory of a Mr Allen, whom must have had a strong connection to the city, he guessed. Khaya took out his phone and snapped a picture of the plate. *It is such a good idea,* he thought to himself. He had been thinking of ways to immortalise his mum and sister.

He watched the kids play, some skating and others doing stunts with their bicycles. He couldn't stop himself from laughing when one of the kids, a little boy who looked Hispanic, fell off his bicycle and rolled over dog poop. Dog poop was always a nuisance. It was why he hated coming to the park, it reeked of it. He couldn't understand why the city wasn't enforcing its pooper-scooper laws, especially in densely populated areas with higher risks of infections. He moved to another section of the park that seemed a bit more tolerable. It was similar to the situation back home. Public spaces were neglected.

He took out a book from his rucksack. It was a

book written by George M. Fredrickson, '*The Black Image in the White Mind*'. He was halfway through the book and found it quite engaging. It told the story of race relations and race theory in the 19th Century America. *It could have been written today*, he thought. Much of the issues discussed in the book remained relevant today in modern-day America, and South Africa for that matter.

He was interrupted by the chirping sound of birds on a nearby tree. He thought birds always looked happy and free. He wished he could be like them, free of all worries, and not having to deal with the gloom and doom that engulfed his life. Nothing seemed to be going right for him at the moment. All efforts to get new funding had been futile. It had become clear that he would be unable to continue with his studies. That much was made clear by his study coordinator, having failed to come up with the required deposit.

His dad had nearly died of a stroke, leaving him with severe impairment to his right side and sensory abilities. His speech had also been impacted. It was heartbreaking to imagine his dad, who had always been independent all his life, now lying helpless in a hospital. The doctors had done an excellent job stabilising him, due largely to the swift intervention of his mum who thankfully knew what to do the very instant she found him slumped on the bedroom floor. He was in intensive care for two weeks, but his doctors had told them that he would be even longer in rehabilitation; this could be anything from few weeks to two months, depending on the level of cognitive impairment.

He agreed with his mum that he should be kept at an inpatient rehabilitation unit within the hospital where he could continue to be monitored by his team of doctors. He felt terrible that he wasn't there for his parents. He had promised his mum that he'd be home as soon as possible. Even though she had tried to persuade him to stay back and focus on his studies, not aware he had hit a financial wall, assuring him that his dad had been stabilised and was in recovery. There was no way he could justify staying back in the face of such a crisis. His parents needed him more than ever. It was his time to give back to them. It was time to go home.

Khaya got up abruptly from the bench. He smiled to himself as some of the birds flew away frantically. Maybe they also have anxieties after all, he murmured, while picking up his rucksack as he walked away from the park.

It was 1995. A new South Africa had emerged.

History had been made a year earlier, as Nelson Mandela was sworn in as the first black president of South Africa and millions had been allowed to vote for the first time. The world was in jubilation, even as echoes of retribution by the blacks permeated the air. There has never been a better time to be a black South African—or an African for that matter.

Khaya had left his home and family three years ago, feeling morose and melancholy, and completely disenchanted with life. Even though he returned home with many questions still unanswered, he had found meaning in caring for the old and sickly—an experience that reshaped his perspective to life. He learnt to embrace himself and to look for support from people who made him feel safe and really cared for. The best place to start was to reach out to everyone he had hurt.

Aunty Nosfundo couldn't hold her anger. His disappearance had disenchanted many who had admired him. She thought he was the most selfish person she had ever met. How could he just turn his back on everyone, his family like that? And after everything that happened. She had been worried sick about him. She had tried to reach out to him on many occasions but wasn't successful, he didn't even bother to return her call. She just couldn't understand what came over him. Did he blame her for his mother's death, or did he also believe that his cousin had something to do with it?

He had no excuse for his behaviour, and was deeply

sorry. He wasn't surprised at her outburst, and in fact, had expected a harsher reaction from her and from others that he had treated so unkindly. He was prepared to put in the work that was required to repair all the broken relationships. The work would have to start with his parents, but he had to call his aunt as soon as he arrived, as there was a high probability of bumping into her at the hospital when he went to visit his dad.

He could understand her displeasure. He knew it had been very difficult for her, for everyone. All the hurt and anger from past two years had been brought to surface with his return back home. She still mourned the loss of her friend, and was still angry at his parents for the way they treated her son during the police investigation. She had felt betrayed.

Khaya apologised to her on the phone and promised to come see her as soon as he left the hospital. He told her that if it was of any comfort, she should know that he never thought for a second that his cousin or his friend, had something to do with the murders. Part of the reason he had been upset with his parents at the time, was because of that. He was disappointed that they pointed fingers at his cousin and his friend. But in time, he came to understand how, in the moment of agony and deep sorrow, one can easily become irrational.

Khaya met with the team of doctors the next day at the rehabilitation unit of the hospital. He had been anxious the whole night, he couldn't wait to see him. The dad was asleep when they got to the hospital, so Khaya and his mum went to see the primary care physician, who was also a family friend. The doctor shared his mum's opinion about the importance of the first three months to his dad's recovery. They needed to keep him under strict monitoring in order to ensure proper restoration of his sensory functions to the pre-stroke levels, but more importantly, to avoid any case of setbacks such as a heart attack or a second stroke.

Khaya would have liked for him to be discharged so he could care for him at home himself, but the mum had declined, much like the other doctors. She had insisted that the discharge plans could only be discussed much later in the rehabilitation, and was dependent on his level of functional impairment.

Just a few minutes into their conversation, the young female nurse who he had met earlier, came into the doctor's office to notify them that the patient was awake and was already asking to see them. Khaya got up excitedly, and followed the nurse, with the mum right behind.

Khaya was overjoyed to see him fully awake and all smiles. He hugged him tightly as both the nurse and his mum watched with broad smiles on their faces. He asked how he was. The dad beamed with so much happiness. The nurse had to stop him repeatedly from jumping out of the bed in excitement.

Even though he was saddened to see him hospitalised, and sickly as it were, he was nonetheless grateful that he was alive and making good progress. His speech, he was told, had improved significantly in past days to everyone's surprise. Khaya could easily understand all that he was saying, and he seemed very coherent too. The doctors had attributed his seemingly quick mental recovery to his years of extensive brain exercise.

Khaya held his dads hand—his experience caring for the sick and elderly back in the States kicked in. He reassured him that he was never going to leave them again. He was home for good. The dad smiled, and told him he wanted him to meet someone, but would have to wait for the next day. Khaya wondered who it was, and told him he would be with him the next day.

———

Khaya was getting impatient. He had been waiting for over an hour for his cousin, who was supposed to meet him at the hospital—they were going to drive to Gugulethu together. He had promised Aunty Nosfundo that he'd be spending the night at her place. It appeared he might have to drive there all by himself. He tried calling him once more. He was just around the corner he said. The taxi was stopping at every spot to pick up passengers. He was sorry for keeping him, and in any case, what was the hurry, he asked.

Aunty Nosfundo was now working at the Bellville hospital in the Northern Suburbs. She was sorry about his dad's illness and glad to know that he was recovering well. He had access to the best care, and was certain he will recover fully in no time. "He's a good man," she said. She promised to go with him the next morning. She had been meaning to visit him since she heard about his illness, but wasn't sure if the wife wanted her to visit. She had been evasive each time she tried to call. Khaya told her it was okay to visit. He was sure the mum and dad would be happy to see her again.

Khaya narrated his experiences in the States to his aunty. He told her about the numerous dreams and the encounter with the woman on the bus. He told her how he had initially dismissed the dreams and thought nothing of it, until it became more rampant and disruptive. He decided to consult a spiritualist that was recommended by his friend and roommate.

Aunty Nosfundo listened attentively as he spoke. He could tell by her reactions that she thought it was some 'heavy stuff'. Khaya had to stop talking at some point because she had suddenly jumped up, being very animated. She was quite alarmed that he didn't reach out to her while he was having those encounters. "Those aren't ordinary dreams, our ancestors had been trying to talk to you," she told him. The woman on the bus was one of their ancestors, she added.

In the past, Khaya would have found her ridiculous, but the way things had unfolded, he was no longer sure what to believe. If there was any meaning to it all, he was ready to find out, and as Bayo had advised, the only place to start was to talk to his aunt. Maybe she could help make sense of it all.

Aunty Nosfundo didn't want him to waste any more time. She wanted them to consult a local spiritualist immediately. She knew a 'Sangoma' in town that they could see the next morning. *She would have to call in sick at work*, she said. Khaya reminded her that he had already consulted a spiritualist in the States, who didn't have much to say besides telling him to return home. He didn't think consulting another would make any difference. Wasn't there something else they could do? She was adamant.

This Sangoma was very powerful, she insisted. It was right that he had come home. *This is a matter that can only be settled by the ancestors,* she told him as they prepared for bed.

It was like being teleported into a mystical world filled with humanoid trees and the grounds covered with glowing mini creatures pulsing with high energy. It was surreal.

But, it didn't feel like that at the beginning. Rather, he had been impressed when they arrived at the Sangoma's office, which was located in the city's ever busy Central Business District (CBD). They were buzzed in by a young and attractive black lady at the reception. She handed them a consultation form to complete, and wanted to know if they'd be paying the consultation fee by cash or card. Khaya looked at his aunty, wondering if they hadn't come to the wrong place. There was no way this could be a place to meet with a spiritualist. It wasn't like anything he'd expected to see at a *Sangoma's* place, in fact, it could have been confused for a doctor's office—much like his parents medical practice.

He was mesmerised by the *Sangoma* in her colourful skirt and shawl, draped across her shoulders with a significant amount of beadworks. The *Sangoma* had asked if he wanted his aunt to stay. He wanted her to. They all sat on a mat spread out in the middle of the room. It was quite a daunting experience for him.

There was a dark cloud hovering around him, and from birth, she said. This darkness was responsible for his entire bad omen. His ancestors are agitated. They have been trying to talk to him. If nothing is done quickly, the bad omens will persist. He wouldn't be able to get a job, or complete any task successfully. He wouldn't be able to find a wife or have children, and may start to develop physical symptoms of fatigue, burning feet, and all sorts.

There were certain cleansings that should have been done for him at birth, and also as a young adult, *the Ulwaluko*—a traditional circumcision and initiation ceremony, from childhood to adulthood. These were required for him to start communicating with the ancestors, and to heal him from all his spiritual problems.

Aunty Nosfundo had to fill in some of the gaps for the *Sangoma* around his birth and childhood. She told the *Sangoma* that he was adopted by his mother's employers, who are whites. She also couldn't tell for sure if any cleansing was done at birth. She wanted to know if it was not too late for the initiation ceremony.

The *Sangoma* insisted it was the only way to reconcile him with his ancestors. The dreams would increase and he may lose his mind unless the *Ulwaluko* is done. She handed him a candle with which he could start using to pray to the ancestors in the meantime, and requested that he returned in a week's time to pick up specially made beads, to be worn on his wrist for protection and spiritual healing. She threw in an extra one for his sick father, it was on the house, she said.

Khaya and his aunt departed for the hospital to visit his father as she had promised. She told him she'd immediately get in touch with his relatives in the village. Such matters are usually handled by the child's father or older males in the family. Women were restricted in matters of *Ulwaluko*. His cousin had done it when he was a teenager, and the process had been handled by his father. But in this case, she wasn't sure his adopted father was in any position to assist, they would have to contact his uncles back in the village. Khaya knew he had to talk to his parents first about it. He couldn't exclude them from such an important aspect of his life.

The parents listened carefully as he tried to explain the dreams, and his encounter with the strange woman. They were not Atheists. His parents were Christians and had raised him as a Christian as well. They were also scientists, which created conflicts at times in their understanding and interpretation of supernatural things. That was the case when Khaya tried to explain his consultation with the *Sangoma*, and how his troubles and bad omens were attributed to his disconnection from his ancestors.

Whilst they appreciated that it was important for him to be connected to his culture, they thought it was excessive for him to want to undergo a traditional circumcision as an adult. They had read of, and seen, many cases of botched circumcision and fatalities arising from such outdated practices. If he was desperate to be circumcised, they could arrange for it to be done for him in a proper medical facility, he might even do it himself, the dad said.

Khaya didn't want to have any confrontation whatsoever. It would defeat the whole purpose of trying to achieve harmony in his life. Instead, he implored them to read a bit more on the subject. He had also done the same. This was an important element of his culture, his heritage. He made them realise that his decision to do the ceremony was not in any way an indictment on them as his parents or a rejection of their ways, but rather an attempt to find harmony in his life.

The physical circumcision was only a part of a bigger initiation ceremony, signifying a cultural evolution of the initiates - a transition from childhood into manhood, a tradition that was widely practiced across Southern Africa. It is a time of prayers to God and the ancestors. The pain endured during the initiation signifies courage and bravery, as the initiates prepare to face the challenges of life.

He had agreed with his aunty to push the *Ulwaluko* further into the New Year. She thought it'd be better to have it in July. She wanted it done as soon as possible, and would ask his elders to expedite the process for selecting the initiation school. They would have to move fast, as the top schools get filled up quickly.

The timing seemed okay. The ceremony usually lasted six weeks all in all. He was sure that'd be enough time for his dad to achieve a near total recovery, and be less dependent on him. It also bought him some time to prepare himself mentally. Truth be told, he was a little apprehensive. His parents were right about cases of failed circumcision, which sometimes could lead to death or worse, partial or total penectomy.

Maybe he didn't have to go through with. He had been praying with the candle and wore the beads provided by the Sangoma, and thought that it should suffice. But then he remembered the words of the Sangoma, initiation it would have to be.

His cousin had reassured him that he had nothing

to worry about, that the instances of failed circumcision were very rare. They were cases nonetheless, Khaya reasoned, and he couldn't just dismiss them. He would have to rely on his uncle's judgement, which made him even jitterier. He hoped that the beads and the candle would keep him safe and bring him good luck during the ceremony.

It was his first Christmas since he returned home, and the first one he'd be spending in a hospital. But as always, Santa showed up. The doctors had great news for them. His dad was making significant progress, and would be discharged soon. It was such delightful news. He could now continue his rehabilitation program at home, after four months in the hospital.

They met with both the physiotherapist and the psychologist to discuss the out-patient treatment plan to be implemented. Khaya would be taking over from his mother as the primary caregiver so she could return back to work. She had already exhausted all her available compassionate leave and had negotiated flexible working hours with the hospital. It was going to be a great start to the year, absent the fact that he would no longer be seeing the beautiful nurse as frequently as before.

He had grown accustomed to her company since that fateful day when his dad had introduced them. He shook her hand, absorbed by her striking beauty, and thanked her for the excellent care for her dad. He thought there was some vibe between them on the day. They had chatted at length thereafter with so much familiarity and no hint of his usual shyness around women, especially beautiful women.

They became good friends, thanks in part to his father's unrelenting manipulations, and spent time at the movies whenever they were both free. Khaya and the nurse worked out that it made his dad happy to see them talking and spending time together, so they continued. However, he wished he wouldn't be too pushy.

Khaya was sure he didn't need any help asking a lady out. He pleaded with his mum to find a way to talk him out of his mischievous plan to hook him up with his nurse. He liked her, but just as a friend. Moreover, he wasn't looking to get into any relationship yet. He had his hands full with more important things to attend to, one of which was the important matter of visiting his Mammi and his sister's killer at the Pollsmoor Prison.

The police had told him they hadn't been able to

get Khwezi to confess to pulling the trigger. He maintained that it was his partner who had shot Mammi and Leanne, but Khaya wouldn't buy it. He was certain the police didn't either. He worked with the theory that Khwezi particularly had not expected to find anyone in the house, and had been surprised by the two ladies. Khwezi must have panicked. He shot the ladies and got rid of the murder weapon. When he was arrested, he did what scums did, tried to save his own skin by pinning the murder on his co-conspirator, knowing that he couldn't dispute his claim.

But Khaya was undeterred. He needed to visit the prison to confront the killer of the two women he loved the most. Khaya needed to know the truth, even if it didn't bring back his loved ones. He would look into his murderous eyes and demand that he confess to firing the shots. He owed him that much.

It was time to visit Pollsmoor.

Pollsmoor Prison, notoriously known for being one of the most dangerous prisons in South Africa. The overcrowded facility located in Cape Town is home to many of the country's most brutal gangsters, and has been the subject of a few international documentaries that aimed to shine light on prison conditions and inmates globally.

One Saturday morning, a little after dawn, Khaya

drove to Pollsmoor Prison in Tokai. It had taken sometime to persuade his mum to stay, he didn't think it was right for her to go with him, after the emotional trauma they had to endure during the trial. This was something he needed to do alone.

He arrived just before 07:00 and there was already quite a long queue of visitors by the prison gate—a prison official he had spoken to earlier had warned—some seated on wooden benches with their little children on their arm waiting for the gates to be opened for visitors. Khaya followed the sign to the parking area, and in no time, joined the long queue.

Pandemonium broke loose as soon as the gates were opened. Suddenly, people appeared from nowhere, pushing into the queue, mothers with babies screaming and fighting. Khaya watched helplessly, holding steady to his position on the now even longer queue. Curses and shouts continued as the prison guards handed out cards with numbers. Yet, no one was allowed into the building. They remained in another queue, on the other side of the gate. Khaya looked at his watch, it was almost 09:00. He calculated that he had been waiting for at least three hours. He was feeling dehydrated.

Some minutes later, they were allowed into the building, and again, they filed into another long queue. It was becoming a charade of long queues.

He was exasperated. He didn't think it'd be this challenging to visit an inmate. It was beginning to feel like they were the prisoners, Khaya thought. Those ahead of him in the queue were being searched—their items taken apart and scrutinized. He was grateful for traveling light, all he had to endure was a mere frisking.

After what seemed like an eternity, he was grateful when they were eventually ushered into the waiting area. His throat was completely dry and hurting. He quickly got himself a bottle of water at a café. He watched some prisoners cleaning as he stood waiting. He thought about all the notorious stories he's heard about the prison—the dangerous prisoners, the brutal guards and the over crowdings. Never in a million years would he have imagined that he'd be standing in the waiting area of the prison, not least visiting Mammi's killer. If only life followed our scripts, he sighed.

Suddenly, he heard a guard call out his name. He followed the female guard to another waiting area where there was, yes, another line of people waiting. This time, in the visitor's room. Not long after, another gate swung open. This was the gate leading to the huge visitors' room.

Khaya was caught off guard as people around him rushed towards the gate. Apparently no numbers were handed out at the waiting room, regular visitors to the prison knew to dash to the gate as soon it is opened. Snapping out of his shock, he squeezed through the crowd into an even bigger room, which was separated by a glass panel. Prisoners were seated on one side of the panel, and on the other side, were all the visitors. He joined the other visitors as they searched frantically for their prisoner.

It didn't matter how long he had thought about it, or prepared for the moment, seeing Khwezi behind the glass panel stopped him in his tracks. Their eyes locked. All the emotions came rushing back. His eyes swelled with tears as he stared at Mammi and his sister's killer. Khwezi held his gaze. He fought back the rage, the urge to scream at him and bang on the glass, anything to let him know that the only thing that would give him any consolation was to be able to strangle him!

Pressing his face against the metal grid of the glass and wanting to be heard over the surrounding noises from other visitors, "Why?" Khaya shouted.

Khaya left Pollsmoore Prison further from any sort of closure he had hoped for. He was upset that the man who was responsible for his family's harrowing pain and endless sorrow, was alive behind bars. It made him sick to his stomach! He wished then that the death sentence could be restored.

Life can be unfair. How he wished he could turn back the hands of time.

It had been over six months that his dad had been discharged. The beads were now a permanent feature on his wrist, candles remain lit every night for prayers before bed, mystical dreams had ceased and he was back in school—having registered with the University of South Africa to complete his Bachelors. He had also stayed in touch with the nurse. Life seemed to be back on the right path for him, it was time to get a paying job. He had exhausted his savings since returning, and now that his dad was feeling much better and less dependent, it seemed to be the appropriate time.

The money had been totally unexpected. His parents had made the big revelation not long after he arrived back in the country. They wanted him to immediately finalise the release paperwork. His parents had taken out a life insurance policy for Mammi the moment she started working with them, and in time, Mammi had completely forgotten about the policy since she had not been responsible for the payment of the premium.

It was the kind of money that could have easily turned his omen around in the States, when he was desperately looking for funding. They had kept it away from him because they didn't want to distract him from his studies, and decided to wait until he was back at home as the sole beneficiary. In fairness to them, they couldn't have known about his financial struggles because he never told them about it, Khaya reasoned. Taking care of Mammi's estate was a nightmare. His mum died intestate— not unusual for many in her circumstance—which made the process even more convoluted.

The whole idea of the "windfall" left him with a mixed feeling. On one hand, he wished he had known about the money while he was searching frantically for funding in the States. Perhaps things may have turned out differently for him, but on the other hand, it was somewhat unsettling that he'd be benefitting from Mammi's death. A woman whose life had been so brutally cut short, all he always dreamt of as a child was to take care of his mother.

The only way to keep Mammi and his sister's memory alive was to immortalise them. And as a first step, he arranged a couple of outdoor wooden chairs, specially handcrafted, with Mammi and his sister's names printed separately on metal plates and attached to the chairs. The chairs were donated to the city to be distributed across the city parks. He invested the rest of the money while he sought advice on how to set up a Foundation, one that would focus on issues of domestic violence and sexual abuse. He knew his mother was committed to those issues in her lifetime. He was sure his sister wouldn't mind it too.

As soon as Khaya had invested the proceeds of the policy, he proceeded on the next plan, getting a job. But with no Bachelor's degree in hand, Khaya mulled over the possibility of approaching his former employer, the Western Cape Horticultural society. He had left on a very good note, even receiving a strong letter of recommendation from his boss – which had helped in his scholarship application at the time. It would be his best bet at least until such time when he had completed his Bachelors and able to find something more fulfilling in the International Relations sphere.

Khaya listened intently to the meteorologist on the evening news. Winter had come early in the year. It was unusually cold in May, and bitingly cold in June. Khaya was worried about the July month. The weather man was not optimistic. All indications pointed towards a record-breaking winter in the country. He knew he couldn't push the initiation ceremony any further. He would have to confront his fears and brave the cold in the mountains.

In any case, he wasn't left with much choice. He had to go ahead with it if he wanted to keep any hope of him and nurse Lesedi alive. They had remained in contact all this time since she moved to Johannesburg to take up a graduate nurse position in one of the top hospitals in the province, while she prepared for her qualifying examination. They would joke around every time she called to check up on her patient, her pet name for his dad, about dating. Lesedi insisted that she was still in love with his father, and considered sacrilegious her culture to date both father and son. Khaya could never outsmart her. It was one of the things he liked about her. Smart and witty, she could talk a dog off a meat truck.

But as tempting as the chase might be, Khaya was well aware of his demons. He didn't plan on jinxing any hope of a future relationship with her until he was done with the *Ulwaluko*. Afterall, a boy couldn't really hope to have a serious relationship with a grown woman, could he? Khaya laughed at himself. He would have to hold off on the offensive for a bit longer.

Midway into the month of June, he received a call from Aunty Nosfundo. She wanted to update him on the preparations for the ceremony and asked if he could come over. Things were moving fast. He was glad that his dad had eventually come round. It felt awkward that the only man he knew as his father couldn't be actively involved in the discussions and preparations for his initiation, as is usually the case— the father decides when a male child has reached the age of maturity and ready for the transition from boyhood into manhood. In his case, the decision to be circumcised was a lot more complicated, much like everything about his life.

The thought of the mountain still gave him the jitters—the cold and even worse, his age. He was almost a decade older than the average initiates who were in their late teens, and it didn't help that his cousin, albeit with good intentions, had told him that the average age of the initiates in early times were over twenty-five years. Apparently in those times, initiates were migrant workers in the mines who needed to work for a while in order to pay for the initiation program.

Khaya left for the village with his aunty and cousin on the last day of the month of June. His uncle had concluded all arrangements with the circumcision school in Cambridge, in East London in the Eastern Cape—the same school his cousin had attended. He was required to undergo some lifestyle changes in preparation for the strict life in the mountain, some deprivation they had called it. He was thankful that staying in the only one star hotel in the village had been cleared by his uncle. He would just have to ensure he stuck to the no alcohol, no sexual intercourse regime, among others. He sent pictures of himself and the hotel to his parents and

Lesedi, who thought he had gotten off lightly.

It was his first time visiting his village and meeting his extended family. He had been slightly embarrassed when his uncle had pulled his ears as he embraced him tightly, calling his mother's name repeatedly instead of his. He took him around the village where he met with his granduncles and grandaunts, a plethora of cousins and several community members. In the village, everyone was family, his uncle had told him. His uncle hadn't been joking, Khaya found out the following day. His sendoff ceremony was a village feast. His aunty and uncle had said they were inviting a few family members but it turned out to be anything but small. "We only slaughtered sheep, wait until *umgidi*, your outing ceremony," Aunty Nosfundo had told him when he complained to her.

The day finally arrived. He was called into a small room where his elders gathered. They all wished him well and commended him for taking the right step. It was the only way he could truly be part of the family. And with that, he departed for the mountains, accompanied by his uncle and cousin.

The debate was getting more heated by the day. This time, the initiates were arguing about the cost of higher education in the country. Khaya agreed that equal access to higher education was critical to the country's transformation agenda. However, he didn't think that the only way to achieve economic development was if higher education was made free as many of his fellow initiates argued. Khaya feared that the argument for mandating free higher education overlooked certain important realities. For starters, government was already grappling with dwindling revenue and unable to provide essential services to the poor. Any sort of tertiary education is an expensive business, never mind a quality one that could compete globally. Achieving the dual objective of a free and quality education seemed challenging if not impossible in the current economic dispensation, Khaya argued.

What he thought what was more practical was a vocational educational system where millions of South Africans could be immediately prepared for professional learning. This would have a greater impact on alleviating the country's huge unemployment and skill crisis. In his opinion, not everyone needed to aspire to the traditional university system.

"My friend, this is South Africa. Not Europe or America," chided one of the initiates who was visibly irritated. "We have had enough of this nonsense. The whites can have their own school if they want, who cares. They can even leave the country," added another. Khaya was perplexed.

He couldn't understand how it suddenly became a race issue. He insisted that ensuring quality and appropriate education had nothing to do with race. But his fellow initiates seemed to have had enough. "Rubbish!" countered one of the youngest initiates. "Didn't you go to that fancy university overseas? But now the rest of us must go to some workshop school. We are tired of listening to your rich boy folktales." Khaya had enough. "Hey, watch your mouth little boy!" he retorted, "We are not mates. You don't get to talk to me like that." Khaya got up and walked away from the group in utter disgust.

The debates didn't always end up ugly as it did that night. In fact, he always looked forward to the dialogues with the other initiates every evening. Even though many of the initiates were a lot younger than he was, he enjoyed engaging in healthy debates around many social and political issues. On rare occasions when tempers flared and things got a little heated, they managed to find a way to resolve matters. He formed strong bonds with some of the initiates—many of whom found his journey interesting and applauded his decision to reconnect with his ancestors—and learnt valuable lessons in humility and cooperation during the process.

Khaya immersed himself into every aspect of the initiation program since he arrived at the circumcision school. And contrary to what he'd expected, he actually found the school interesting. Perhaps a lot had to do with the guidance from his cousin. He was grateful that he was there with him, especially those first few days during the circumcision. His parents would have been impressed by the professional care he received from the traditional surgeon and nurses, the *imcimbi* and the *amakhankatha* on site, he thought to himself wryly.

The daily solitary walks in the mountain provided him the opportunity to reflect on his life journey. He fell in love with the serenity and virginity of the mountains, while pretending with stick in hand, that he was an ancient forager. There were moments when he could have sworn that he saw flashes of his ancestors in the hills. It was an exhilarating experience that none of his younger companions could understand.

The initiation period went quickly. On the eve of their departure from the mountain, the elders reminded them of their new responsibilities to society and their respective families. Even though they may have successfully gone through the initiation process, they did not automatically become 'men'. Rather, it was the beginning of a process, a transition into manhood, and was expected to conduct themselves in the ways of respectable men.

It was exactly what held him back from complaining about the extravagant *umgidi*—his outing ceremony. Aunty Nosfundo had been right. The send off ceremony was child's play. It felt like the entire village had been invited to the *umgidi* ceremony. Yes, he was now a custodian of tradition, a full-fledged man, and he should be paying more attention, but this was well over his head. He scanned around for his aunty.

"How much longer do I really need be here?" he asked as soon as he could pull her aside. He was hoping he could leave as early the day after the ceremony. He had been gone for over six weeks, and had been incommunicado for most of it, no thanks to the school's strict policy of no cellular phones. He was happy that the initiation ceremony had been successful. He desperately needed to get back to the life he was more comfortable with.

It was a beautiful Monday morning. Khaya smiled as he hummed along to the blaring music on his iTunes. Not even the notorious Cape Town rush hour traffic could dampen his spirit. The moment was suddenly interrupted by a call, it was Lesedi.

Even though he knew better not to pick a call while driving, he picked anyway. "Hello, lady" said Khaya as he fumbled around on the phone to put it on speaker.. She had sent him a short message on his phone earlier and decided to call when he hadn't responded. She would be in Cape Town the coming weekend and wanted to know if he had any plans. She would also like to come say hello to her patient, she added. Of course, he would be happy to be her chauffer for the weekend, Khaya joked. His day couldn't get any better. He was delighted that he'd be seeing her again. Since returning from the mountain, he had been to Johannesburg a few times to see her, although he often hid under the cover of travelling for work.

He had joked with his cousin that he needed to confirm if indeed his omens were starting to change for the better. He had gotten his old job back, but the litmus test would be if Lesedi begun to have endless dreams about him. His cousin had laughed. He hoped they would be good dreams.

Khaya was certain she was having good dreams. He had asked her during one of his visits if it was safe for him to be taking her out. He didn't want some jealous boyfriend attacking him in public, he told her jokingly. It was a line so hackneyed that she just gave him one of her 'signature' looks for when she thought someone was fishing. It was all he needed to know. He had learnt never to disrupt the flow of the river.

He really liked her. He found that he could tell her anything. She always seemed to have a way with words. She said the right things at the right time, and had a sense of humour unlike anything Khaya had ever seen before.

He remembered sharing with her his concerns about the circumcision, and particularly his fear of a penile deformity. He was worried about cases of participants being left with permanent scarring and in some cases, penises becoming gangrenous that they just drop off. Lesedi had laughed so hard that he actually got irritated that she'd found his genuine fears funny. But seconds later as soon as she had stopped laughing, she told him on the bright side, that even if his penis were to somehow just drop off, it might just open up a new world for him as a man of the cloth. The best part was he'd never have to worry about backsliding!

He was grateful that things were starting to move in the right direction since his return. He had rebuilt his relationship with his parents, reconciled with his ancestors and had confronted Mammi's killer in prison. He had finally established a Trust in a joint name for his mother and sister, which really made him happy. He also registered with the University of South Africa to complete his Bachelor's degree. And while life was also great with Lesedi, there was just one more thing to do. He had pushed it back for as long as possible. He knew that if they were to continue on the process of healing, they needed to act on the matter of the house, and what to do with Mammi and his sister's belongings.

No one had lived in the house since the incident. His parents spent some time in Franschhoek and later moved to Bloemfontein to spend some additional time with his mother's parents. They eventually had to buy a new place in the north of the city upon their return back to Cape Town three months later. They had not been able to bring themselves to going back to the old house, choosing to leave its care in the hands of a caretaker agent. Khaya had been talking to Lesedi about his plans. She agreed with him. They couldn't just ignore it. They had to take a decision and best to do it soon and move on.

As Khaya stepped into the house, he saw his parents by the pool outside. He was tempted to join them. It was scorching hot, but he had a more pressing matter to discuss. He hated to be the one to break up such a rare moment of happiness, but it was either now or never, he told himself as he walked over to them.

Khaya dragged one of the chairs closer to the edge of the pool. He told them there was something he needed to discuss with them. The mother adjusted her swimming cap and pulled herself out of the pool. She grabbed a towel, wiped her face, and with her usual cheekiness, asked if he was about to marry the nurse? "No mum!" Khaya exclaimed. "I have told you countless times that we are just friends and this isn't about her anyway" he added. By this time, the dad had also come out of the pool, dragging a seat beside him. "So what's it about?" The dad asked.

He told them it was about the old house. He knew it was uncomfortable for them— it was for him as well he told them. He thought it was about time he cleared out Mammi's belongings and if they didn't mind, he would also like to do the same with his sister's too, he added. He also asked what they wanted to do about the house. They just couldn't abandon the house forever and continue running municipality bills and other housekeeping bills. They were aware of the increasing damages to the house. The caretaker had warned that if nothing gets done quickly about renting out the house or selling it, the building would dilapidate further. Houses needed humans in order to breathe, the caretaker had said. Khaya wanted their permission to either rent it out or find a buyer, whichever comes first.

Surprisingly, his parents agreed with him. He had expected them to demand a bit more time to think about it, but here they were—all happy for him to do whatever felt right. They didn't want anything to do with the house. They said they were happy for him to also get rid of his sister's belongings. They would rather sell the house immediately, and would discuss it with their lawyer. He hugged his mother. He knew how hard it was for her, for all of them. They had never spoken about it as a family but each one knew how much it hurts, but more importantly, they knew how much they all cared. They were all they had left.

There was just one small matter left. Khaya had also wanted to discuss his plans of moving out. He had been thinking of getting his own place now that things were a little more settled at home and his dad a lot more independent. He had moved in with them upon his arrival from the States, as natural as it appeared, but it was his own way of saying he was sorry for being such a pain, and for abandoning them when they all needed each other the most. He moved in to make up for all those lost times, while he was overseas caring for strangers. However, judging by the emotions of the moment, after the 'heavy-lifting' on the topic of the house, he was worried that talking about moving out may be a little too much to bear. He decided to postpone the conversation— lest they misconstrue his actions as another attempt at bolting. But if wanted any progress with Lesedi, he knew they'd have to have the talk sooner than later.

He knew he couldn't do it alone. Not even with the beads and candles. He would need a lot more. Khaya turned to the one person that he knew could hold his hands through the ordeal. It would be a lot more bearable if she went with him.

His parents had commented on several occasions on their growing closeness and wanted to know if they were officially an 'item'. He had told them they were just friends— which was the truth—even though he knew that a lot remained unspoken between them.

He didn't want to make any assumptions and wanted to thread very softly. He was still healing from the scar from his experience with Simone. He would rather wait for things to develop organically, but if anything, he was certain they were both happy. He didn't think she'd be flying so often if she didn't care as much.

Lesedi felt honoured when he asked her to accompany him to the house. She knew how much it meant to him and would not give up the privilege to share the moment with him. *It was an opportunity to bond with him*, she thought to herself. If she could have accompanied him to the mountains, she would have.

The memories hit him hard the moment he stepped into the house. He was glad the caretaker had arrived early as promised—he had little tolerance for people who keep him waiting for no reason. He looked around for a while, taking in the moment. It had been over three years. The last moments came rushing back—the scene at the house, the ambulances, police, neighbours coming in droves, and the days following. The house had been like a torturous hell. All he wanted was just to leave, but someone had to stay back to attend to the funeral matters and sympathisers. His parents had been advised to vacate the house and stay in a guest house during the whole time.

He braced himself for the uphill task ahead. He grasped Lesedi's hand as they both made their way to the entrance where the caretaker was waiting. "Are you okay?" She asked. "Yes I am. I think so" Khaya responded. She squeezed his fingers in a reassuring way. He was glad that he asked her to accompany him, even though it wasn't the ideal way to introduce the one you care about to your past, or your world for that matter.

They were greeted with the smell of an old and abandoned house. It felt really odd that the house that was once filled with so much life, had turned into a ghost of its old self. It was quite dark inside. *The caretaker should have switched on the lights*, he thought to himself, as he flicked on the switch in the doorway.

Most of the furniture was covered in plastics. Family pictures still lined the walls of the living room. He blew off the dust from a few, as he took them off their hooks. They were baby pictures of his sister and himself. He passed them over to Lesedi, who chuckled at a picture of him, half naked and running around with a rugby ball almost half his size. There was another picture of his sister fighting him for his ice cream. It was such a funny photograph. They both had cream splattered all over their tiny faces. He reckoned they must have been four or five years old when it was taken. Lesedi put them away in the duffel bag that they brought along.

He uncovered the chaise lounge—it was his dad's favorite chair. He stood by the chair for a few seconds, reliving those times in the evenings, and on some weekends, when his father sat in the chair with the TV remote or a newspaper, lost in his own world. There were only two places he knew, where he readily immersed himself, it was in his operating theater and on his favourite chaise lounge. Those days are long gone. He hoped that at least he'd still be able to go back to his medical practice someday.

Khaya walked towards the patio. He noticed the sliding door was locked. The caretaker was nowhere in sight, so he just opened up the drapes and pressed his face onto the glass door. He looked through the large patio. It was filled with character and history. It was where it had all begun for him. His parents had told anyone who cared to listen, about how he ended up living in the house with them, and how he became their second child. But the one version that stayed with him the most, and even more so now, was that of Mammi.

She had told him about her migration to the city from a small village in the Eastern Cape with absolutely nothing but hope, and about how her sister, aunty Nosfundo had been her guardian. She had struggled to find a lasting paying job and when she fell pregnant with him, things became even more difficult for her, emotionally and financially. She feared that her sister was also getting frustrated as she increasingly became a bigger burden on her. But the heavens had bigger plans for her, she told him. Shortly after giving birth to him, aunty Nosfundo found a job. One of her bosses in the hospital had also just had a baby. Their domestic worker had left for her hometown and they were desperately in need of a help— a live in helper. The timing couldn't be better for the two struggling sisters with two infants to feed. Thembeka jumped at the opportunity, but without disclosing to the new employers that she also had a 10-month-old baby.

She didn't have to, for as long as she could, she left the child at a makeshift crèche close to aunty

Nosfundo's house in the township every day while she was away during the week. Aunty Nosfundo had volunteered to help her out after hours. She had arranged with her supervising officer at the hospital to stay on the morning shift for as long as possible. It was a very hectic period for all of them. Aunty Nosfundo was particularly stretched thin, with her own child and work to think of, and now the added responsibility of another child. It was obvious that with such an arrangement, it was not sustainable. The Johnson's were also irritated that Thembeka would often take time off work during the day at very short notice to attend to 'family matters'. They wondered what was going on exactly.

Things came to a head when the makeshift crèche closed down abruptly. The owner claimed the crèche was not profitable and had turned the crèche into a pub, known as a *Shebeen* locally, overnight. Thembeka had to make a difficult decision. She had to decide if to resign immediately or to come out clean to her employers. She chose neither, instead she appeared at her work the next morning with a one-year-old baby on her back.

Mammi always told him how grateful she was that they took him in and treated him just like their second child.

Lesedi remained captivated by the house—both by

its grandiosity and the sadness that filled the air. She imagined what it must have felt like growing up in the house. He had told her countless stories of his childhood days, many of which included memories of the house. It was easy to picture him in the house, it was surreal. She looked at the family pictures. She had seen a replica in the Johnson's new home but not this many collections of the different stages in the family history. She noticed, however, that Khaya's biological mother was not in many of the pictures except a few where the kids were toddlers.

Khaya made his way to the kitchen. He knew it was probably just his mind playing tricks on him, but both times that he'd been in the kitchen since the incident, it just felt like the kitchen came alive and he could hear Mammi doing the dishes. It was the most unsettling feeling ever, he told Lesedi as he tried to describe the sensation. He wondered if she could feel it too, and if it had anything to do with Mammi's spirit lingering?

Khwezi had tried to apologise to him at the prison. He said he had not intended for anyone to get hurt on that day. He never would have knowingly harmed his mother. Even though they were no longer in a relationship, he still liked her and would never hurt her. It was his stupid friend he said. They had been caught off guard. He hadn't expected that she'd be working on that day, or to find anyone in the house for that matter. In all the time he'd known her, she had always spent her weekends with her sister in the township, and later with him when they started dating, and the Johnson's have also mostly spent their weekends away.

He had good intelligence, well not so good in hindsight, that the house was going to be empty on that particular weekend. All he had to prepare for was the dog and maybe that of the neighbours too. He knew the Johnson's sometimes left their dog behind when they went away on weekends, so he had come prepared with an extra treat to 'silence' the dog. He didn't know that his co-conspirator was armed on that day, and would go wild, claiming he panicked as soon as he realised there were people in the house.

Khaya suddenly felt the urge to say a short prayer for Mammi's soul right there in the kitchen. He prayed that her spirit would find peace, and would rest with her ancestors. Lesedi had suggested a more robust ceremony to cleanse the house and send off Mammi and his sister's spirits peacefully, but he wasn't about to go through another bout of cultural extravaganza, he had told her. All he wanted to do was to clear the house and make it ready for the new buyers or tenants as the case may be. He reckoned the short prayer would suffice for now.

They moved along to the bedrooms. The master bedroom was huge. It had also doubled as his dad's library. He couldn't help notice that some books had been taken out of the library. He could see the huge gap in between the books, as some of them had fallen over. Khaya wondered if his dad had taken the books. He was aware that his dad and mum had taken most of their personal belongings previously, especially clothing, but most other heavy items had stayed. He made a mental note to ask him or the caretaker later on. He knew how pedantic his dad was with his books. He easily lost his cool if he found any of his books not placed neatly in the shelf, and in the right order.

He walked closer to the shelf, unwrapped the plastic cover, and without hesitation, started to rearrange the books. It was like a giant domino, once he started with one book, the remainder of the books started falling apart. Lesedi couldn't help laughing as she joined him in the exercise. At least it seemed like a much needed therapy for both of them. "You know, if there was anything my father couldn't live without, besides his wife, it was his books," Khaya said, as they cleaned and stacked the books in their right places in the shelf.

They passed through the adjoining door to his mother's room. Everything was covered. Lesedi walked towards the paintings on the wall. She had always been a lover and collector of great local pieces. She lifted the makeshift vails on many of the pieces. The one depicting the beauty of South Africa's Highveld caught Lesedi's attention. It was a masterpiece by one of South Africa's well-known artist. She blew some of the trapped dusts off the picture. They exited the room, and made their way to the next room down the hall. It was the guest room.

It was also where the linens were stored. Directly opposite the guest room was Khaya's room. Lesedi couldn't wait to see what his room looked like. She was sure she could tell what sort of a child he was just by looking at his room. The room was nothing like an average teenager's room. There were no nude pictures of super models hanging around his wall, nor were there interesting magazines to flip through. Khaya picked up a few items from his reading table. The rest of his items would be in storage until he gets his own appointment.

The last bedroom was further down the hall.

It had an old ribbon stuck on the door. Lesedi guessed it must be his sister's room. Khaya lifted the Christmas ribbon. It was still firmly attached just to the door. They all had ribbons on their doors at one point during Christmas many years ago when he was a little child, and while the rest of them had taken them off, she was the only one who refused to take hers off. He recalled the times when he'd piss her off by trying to snap the ribbon whenever she was mean to him, and the ensuing fight and screams that always irked their parents.

He looked at it now, snapped it off just as they entered the room, and handed it over to Lesedi. He would cherish it for as long as he lived. Her room was her castle from where she filled the house with her beautiful voice each time she sang. He took a moment, trying hard to imagine her singing again. Lesedi looked through the window—she could see a part of the garden, which was now overgrown. He opened her wardrobe. Everything would go to charity. Khaya joined Lesedi by the window. The countless times he had kicked his soccer ball at her window. It was too much to bear. Lesedi threw her hands around him just as he sunk into the bed in tears. No words were needed.

The next stop was the back flat, Mammi's apartment.

Lesedi had suggested to take a break. They could come back another time to finish up. She thought they had achieved an awful lot for the day, amidst all the emotional turmoil. But Khaya thought otherwise. He wanted to get it over and done with it. It wasn't the sort of pain he thought he could endure twice.

He had let her aunt dispose Mammi's items that were left at her place, only keeping her cellular phone and handbag that had been returned by the police shortly after the case was closed. The remainder of her belongings would also be given to charity except for the ones that he decided to keep for himself.

If he thought the kitchen in the main house was filled with Mammi's spirit, her little apartment was alive with her soul. This was the room where Khaya spent special moments with Mammi, the place where he took many naps, sometimes in her arms, on her legs, and many other times, spending the night. It was the place where she managed to teach him the ways of his ancestors—away from the prying eyes of his second family. In this room, she only spoke to him in Isixhosa and demanded that he replied in it. It was where he would later be told the story of how he came to live in the main house. It was where Mammi retired to every day, exhausted, for over eighteen years. It was her fortress. It was where she found peace. It was where Khaya came to say his final goodbye.

Even though he no longer had the dreams, there was no passing day that he hadn't thought of her. As he stood right in the middle of the apartment, he again wished for a moment that losing her was just all a long bad dream.

He could feel the guilt coming back. He beat himself up many times for not spending enough time with her when he could have. He was too self-involved to take a moment to feel her pain. How as a child, he was too busy living his privileged life, sometimes ashamed and critical of Mammi, and how as a teenager, was too bitter with everyone, with the world—too lost in his own internal conflict to realise how much his mother was hurting.

"Who are these people?" Lesedi asked, as she handed a few photographs she picked up from the table to him. He looked at the first photograph, it was a picture of aunty Nosfundo , his two cousins, Mammi and himself in Gugulethu. The picture was taken in Aunty Nosfundo's house on one of the weekends they spent in the township. Another picture was of Mammi's *Mkhulu*. He never met his great-grandfather but knew enough about him from Mammi. He returned the photographs and asked that she drop them in the bag with the rest of the items.

He pulled the wardrobe handle. It was locked. He wondered if the caretaker had locked it, but surely not. He had left every other wardrobe unlocked. Khaya looked around the room, "The key must be somewhere in the room," he told Lesedi. They both searched around frantically for some minutes but were unsuccessful. "I may have to force it open" said Khaya, as he looked around for anything strong enough.

He stopped for a moment, and in a trance like posture, pleaded quietly in his mind that Mammi would direct him to where she kept the keys. He was about to leave the room to go find some tools in the kitchen, when his eyes fell upon a set of trays in a tower like form, set up on the dressing table. Something in him nudged him towards the table, and just as he lifted the trays, he found tucked underneath was a set of keys. He was spellbound! Lesedi had no inkling whatsoever of what just unfolded.

Khaya grabbed the keys, laughed out loud, so loud. Lesedi was bowled over, watching him as he dangled the keys in her face. He tried one of the keys on the wardrobe door. The lock turned at the third attempt, and he flung the door open to a huge sigh of relief, wondering if to tell her what just happened. He thought against it. He didn't want to freak her out.

He carefully combed through her wardrobe, grateful for once, for Mammi's minimalist nature. He found some folded notes under a pile of clothes in the wardrobe. He had not expected to find a diary, Mammi wasn't into the art of writing, but there was a bundle of notes, and he was excited to find them.

He unfolded one of the notes. It was some sort of a journal— dated and seemed to be addressing her grandfather. He guessed she must have intended to send it to him at some point and never got to. She wrote about her first few days in Cape Town. How she missed him and her friends in the village. She wanted to know how her brothers and his bicycle business was doing. Khaya lowered himself onto the bed as he unfolded the second note, there she complained about not finding a job and finding it hard surviving in the city. She was wondering if she should return home. She asked if he remembered her friend, Nosfundo whose parents lived three houses from theirs in the village. She went on to tell him how supportive she has been. Khaya read further while Lesedi went through the rest of the wardrobe.

Suddenly, Khaya got up from the bed, folded the notes and asked that they leave. Lesedi was taken aback at the abruptness of his decision. There was still the other half of the wardrobe to go through. Khaya told her he was done and led her out of the room. He would instruct the caretaker to take all the stuff into storage. Lesedi watched in utter disbelief. His face was as pale as that of someone who had just seen a ghost. She wondered what had caused him to flee the apartment. She had a hunch it had to do with the notes he was reading, but decided not to pry.

They drove back to his parent's house in silence. He was visibly angry and shaken. She kept asking if he was okay, and he kept giving the same response, 'I am fine, dear. Just a little thing, don't want to talk about it now". It was not the way she had envisaged the day to end, but she was glad that she was there to support him.

———

Lesedi was Sotho. Her ancestors identified as southern Sotho, whom together with the northern Sotho people, make up the second largest ethnic group in South Africa. Her parents migrated to Cape Town from Bloemfontein in the early 70s. Lesedi was born in Cape Town in the year in 1980. She was the only child.

Lesedi grew up in the city, in the old middle class suburb of Kenilworth in Cape Town— famous for the Kenilworth Racecourse. She was an excellent student who took little notice of her extraordinary beauty and had little time for boys during her student days—no thanks to her strict and old fashioned parents. She was known by her friends as the 'old soul' for being far too wise for her age and her peers.

Ever since she was a little child, Lesedi knew she wanted to be a medical doctor. Unlike kids her age, she was never weary of hospitals or doctors' offices. She would insist that her parents take her to see a doctor at the slightest sneeze. She never missed a dental appointment, and always dressed up in varieties of medical attires during dress up days all through primary school. 'Show and Tell' days, were her favourite school activities. Underpinning her desire to be a medical doctor was her love for people. She was a very caring and loving child.

It was therefore devastating to everyone who knew and loved her, when she couldn't get admission into any of the universities to study Medicine after her Matric (high school). Her parents tried hard to persuade her to consider going for a degree in Information Technology (IT). They had heard from many of their friends that IT was the future, and all the kids were rushing to study IT. But Lesedi was not one to be swayed. She decided to enroll at the National College of Nursing instead. She reckoned if she couldn't get in to study Medicine now, she would take the longer route, be a registered nurse first and then go on to be a medical doctor. At least, she'd still be living her dream of being in the medical industry.

Four years of nursing school went by quickly for Lesedi. It was also where she experienced her first heartbreak. She had a crush on one of her educators. He was one of the youngest educators in the college. He had a PhD and taught the clinical components of nursing. Lesedi was very attracted to him, not because of his looks, at least she told herself that, but because of his intelligence. He was very popular among the students, not least the female students. Lesedi managed to keep her obsession to herself for the first year of college. She ran out of luck in her second year when her friends forced her to attend his farewell party. He had told them he was moving back to his home in Botswana to start a new position as the head of one of the country's topmost Nursing Colleges.

They had all been heartbroken at the news, especially Lesedi. She had never had a crush on any one before, and didn't know what to do. She was also too scared to confide in her friends. They had always teased her about boys, and would come up with stories of some male students who liked her and all. She was never interested. She feared that if she told them about her secret crush, they might judge her wrongly, so she kept her secret to herself.

She judged herself for a very long time after the farewell party. She asked herself repeatedly if she sent out some wrong signals during the party or if by some evil machinations, he had seen through her, and read her mind that day. The brief encounter, as she loved to refer to it, started with a casual chat at the party. It was the first time outside of the college that she was having a conversation with him. He must have picked up on her nervousness and took advantage of it. He was apparently more experienced in such matters as she found out much later, albeit too late.

He had told her he would still be around for a few more weeks before moving finally to Botswana. He needed to sort out some matters, and take care of his furniture and all. After a few phone calls and phone messaging, Lesedi agreed to meet him for drinks. He was as charming as she imagined. It was a new feeling for her, and quite intriguing. The drinks became more frequent. She hated that she kept it from her close friends. He told her he was a very private person and also didn't want their friendship making the school gossip rounds. He was easy to fall in love with. He made her feel very special. It was a very good feeling, until it wasn't.

It was hard to tell for sure which hurt the most, the betrayal, her stupidity or the shame she endured once her friends found out. But just like she's done all her life, she picked herself up once more, and focused all her energy into her studies. *Whoever said anything about beginners luck couldn't have been more wrong when it came to matters of the heart,* she chided herself.

Lesedi had just started her clinical experience at Groote Schuur hospital in Cape Town when she was assigned to Dr Johnson. She had been told by her supervisor that Dr Johnson was a VIP patient. Not only was he staff of the hospital but was also one of the best Anesthetists in the country. She was considered lucky to have such a high profile patient as her first patient care position.

Unlike what her patient may have hoped for, she was not immediately smitten when she eventually met Khaya. He was not particularly attractive, and in fact, appeared a few inches shorter than her. Lesedi liked tall and lean men. He was short and chubby. However, what mattered most was that she felt she had known him for a much longer time.

Dr Johnson couldn't stop talking about his son in the States, and often teased her about him and how they'd make a great couple. She would smile and tell him stories about her imaginary boyfriend, and how he wouldn't be happy to hear that her favourite patient was trying to 'hook' her up with his son. But it didn't seem to work on him. Whenever his wife visited, he would go on and on again, asking her if she didn't think their son and the nurse would make a great pair?

She could tell how much they both miss their son. She had caught glimpses of sadness on their faces whenever they talked about him. Mrs Johnson had told her that she wished he'd call more often even if he didn't want to return home. Dr Johnson's sickness had been hard on the wife. It's been very tough trying to stay strong. She didn't think she could survive it if anything happened to him, not after losing their daughter.

Lesedi had heard from the gossip mill in the hospital that they had raised their helper's child from birth and was their second child—well, their only child now. She had also heard that he was a troubled child and had dropped out of university due to drugs and all sorts. He had also abandoned his family shortly after Mammi's death and left the country without trace. She knew the Johnsons were taking a lot of strain and were very fond of him, even if all she heard was true. Dr Johnson definitely thought highly of him, enough to want to marry her off to his wonderful black son.

The entire ward was abuzz with the news of the Johnsons' son's return. It was all Dr Johnson spoke about the entire week. It was hard not to be equally excited. She found herself looking forward to meeting him, and even told some of her friends about this great return.

As fate would have it, she was not on duty the first day Khaya visited the hospital. She only got to meet him the following day when he returned with his mother. She watched with great delight as the highly esteemed Dr Johnson beamed with the excitement of a little boy. He couldn't wait to introduce them. She laughed and told him how she had looked forward to meeting him. "I feel like I have known you for a very long time actually" Lesedi said. He smiled back at her, as he held on to hand—for a bit too long she thought. "Is that right'? he replied tongue-in-cheek.

Dr Johnson remained in the hospital for three more weeks during which Lesedi and Khaya got to see each other a number of times, including a few drinks outside of her shifts. She found that what he lacked in looks, he made up for in personality. He was soft spoken, charming in a way, sensitive and had a big heart. She also discovered that he was still struggling with his losses, much like his parents. If anything, she didn't see him as the mean, selfish son, who abandoned his parents. She was getting to like him more each passing day. But she remained skeptical. She hasn't had any serious dates since her last experience in nursing school, and was not sure she was ready to get involved in a serious relationship as yet.

However, things were moving fast and slow at the same time. They shared so many things in common. They shared similar taste in music and both loved to dance, admittedly he was a better dancer that she was. He was also an avid reader of everything written, just as much as she was. She was also sure that they enjoyed each other's company, and felt at ease sharing personal stuff with each other.

As time went by, she realised she may be warming up to the idea of a relationship; however it didn't look like he wanted to take things to the next level. Even though He would make jokes about them being together, and how his parents would love for them to be together, he didn't make any advances himself.

She couldn't understand why he was holding back. Some of her friends had suggested 'nudging' him, but she didn't want to have to prompt him, or any man for that matter. She was old school, and believed that a man should ask a woman out—explicit or otherwise, and not the other way around. He had left her even more confused when he had asked her to accompany him to their old house, a place that held so much pain. That was something you do with family or someone special—she thought it signaled his trust and reliance on her support. Maybe he just wanted them to be friends. *Maybe he didn't like her as much as she did, or maybe there was a secret girlfriend in the States waiting*, she thought to herself.

Khaya knew he had to put aside the anger and disappointment that he was feeling as soon as they arrived back at his parents' home. He didn't want his parents to think it was a really bad idea going to the house, and also didn't want them to get upset either. Intsead, he put on a cheery look—much to Lesedi's surprise, but she was getting used to his many idiosyncrasies.

They had planned to have lunch at his parent's house. The mum had made lasagna—her favourite dish, but Khaya had a change of mind. He thought they should go out instead to a restaurant, partly because he felt guilty the way things turned out at the old house. He wanted to make it up to her. But Lesedi didn't want to go out to a fancy restaurant unrefreshed. She pleaded with him to take her home so she could freshen up and have a change of clothes. She suggested maybe he should do the same given the long day in the old house. He smiled. Women would never stop fascinating him. *They just have to order you around*, he thought to himself.

They made a quick stop at Lesedi's parent's house. He had met both her parents on many occasions. They were very nice people. The first time he met her mum, he had joked with her that she could easily pass as her mother's twin. She had teased him back, asking if he was suggesting that she looked old. He liked her parents. He discussed politics with his dad. They were both frustrated with the ruling party. The father thought the party had veered away from all it stood for during the struggle days. Khaya felt the same way, but was there a better alternative, he argued.

He secretly checked his watch again, careful not to be caught doing so by her father. He was worried that they may not get a seat at the restaurant once the evening reservations rolled in. He had thought she was just going to have a quick one, but as soon as she stepped out, it was obvious why it had taken her so long. There was nothing quick about the way she looked. She looked stunning in her short summery dress. Instinctively, Khaya looked at himself, thinking he could have done a much better job himself.

The restaurant was getting crowded as they arrived. Thankfully, he had managed to get a reservation while he waited for her to get ready. It was a good decision seeing how quickly the restaurant filled up just before 18:00 in the evening. They got a seat outside, overlooking the ocean. It was a beautiful summer evening, exactly what he needed after an emotionally packed day.

After dinner, Khaya suggested that they took a short walk along the ever busy stretch of road. They crossed to the other side of the road, and walked towards the beach. They sat on one of the benches by the kiddies play area. Khaya reached into his pocket and brought out a rumpled note. He handed it to Lesedi. She recognised the note from back at the old house earlier that day. Khaya urged her to read it.

Mid-way into the note, she suddenly gasped. She knew that whatever it was in the note that made him upset must have been some quite revealing, but never could she have guessed that it was that shattering. She hugged him tightly. "I am so sorry. I had no idea. Oh my, how horrible!" She repeated to him. He told her he never knew Mammi went through such a horrible ordeal. It started to make sense why she was so passionate about matters of sexual violence.

Khaya starred far into the sunset, and in a whisper, asked her the one question that's occupied his mind since he read the note. He asked if she thought it was possible that he was the child of rape. He had always suspected that there was more to the story than what Mammi had told him about his father. He had wondered why she never bothered to be interested in tracking him down, or why she didn't want him to do so either. Both her and his aunt, had told him he was probably dead anyway or if not, didn't want to be found. He probably has a new family in Swaziland. He found it odd that there was not even a photograph of him. The only image he had was the one painted by Mammi—and to his mind, looked like every black man in the township.

Lesedi didn't know what to say. She wasn't even sure if he wanted her to even respond. She just held onto his hands, following his gaze into the sunset. She was scared to think of the possibility of what he was asking. She got up from the seat, pulling him up as well in the process. He followed her lead, stopping just before the wet sand.

She turned around slowly, throwing her arms around his neck with her face pressing into his. He looked into her eyes. It was the most intimate they'd done since meeting. Then she spoke to him in the sweetest voice he's ever heard all his life. She wanted him to know that it didn't, and shouldn't matter, how he was conceived. What mattered was that he was raised in love, and blessed with parents and people who adored him. It was time to look forward, she told him, as she held him tight and kissed him passionately.

It was the turning point in their relationship.

———

Khaya was delighted about the progress his dad was making with his health. His physician had been very positive during their last visit. He thought the risk of a more severe stroke was greatly diminished. His mobility had also greatly improved, gaining increased use of his limbs and muscles. He was truly a fighter. His mother was equally relieved. She had been back to full time work since Khaya returned home. The family was healing and moving forward together. It was exactly what he had come home to achieve, and was grateful that it all seemed to be working out well. His life was coming together nicely again. He thought it was a perfect time for a family holiday.

Christmas presented the perfect opportunity. On one lazy weekend, Khaya sat around the house with the parents. He brought up the idea of going on a holiday. He thought it'd be great if they all spent the holidays at their vacation home just like the old times. He had already arranged with the agent to block out a couple of days. His parents liked the idea. The mum asked if he'd like to invite Lesedi. She was like family, she said while patting his shoulder. Khaya looked at his father, who nodded in agreement.

Not many families took the practice of time-together-as-family during the holidays as religiously as Lesedi's family. They had always spent Christmas together as a family ever since she was a child, she had told him on several occasions. It was a family ritual that no one had dared to break. He didn't want to be the one to ask her to break a family tradition. Even though he had liked the idea of her coming along when his mum suggested it, he knew there was no point asking her if he already knew what her response would be. He had planned it as a family get-away anyway, they would have to keep it that way.

Aniston in December was always very busy. The roads were a nightmare. His parents had always preferred to go during off-season, when it was quieter, and the beaches were less congested with locals and foreigners. They arrived in Aniston shortly after sunset on the eve of Christmas. It had taken him over five hours driving down from Cape Town, an hour more than usual. He stopped by the agent's office to pick up the keys to the house. She confirmed that everything was in order and was happy to see everyone again.

As he approached the house, Khaya noticed a

car parked in the driveway. The car looked very familiar, too familiar he thought. "It couldn't be," he whispered, turning to his dad who was seated beside him. He shrugged, acting ignorant. Khaya turned around to his mum, who also tried to avoid his stare.

He parked beside the car, and rolled down his window. "Surprise!"She shouted from her open window. He was still spellbound. Nothing came out of his mouth as he tried to speak. *How did they manage to pull this off? And who did?,* He thought to himself. But nothing mattered at that moment; she was there, in Aniston. Somehow, she had broken her family tradition for him, which was the only thing that mattered. He rushed out of the car just as she stepped out of hers. He picked her up, and spun her around until he was dizzy. His parents looked on, happy for the part they played in making such a happy moment happen.

On Christmas day, Khaya decided to take Lesedi to see the Waenhuiskrans Cave. They had all been surprised when she told them she had never been to the cave, even though she had come close to doing so when she visited Aniston in the past. Khaya thought it was unforgivable for anyone to come to Aniston and not visit the legendary cave. He decided they'd take a walk to the cave in the evening when it was much cooler, and at low tide.

It was less than 30 minutes from the house, and he didn't have much time anyway as she was scheduled to leave the following day. He also thought it would be the perfect place to have the talk.

Earlier that morning, Khaya had gone to his mum. His hunch was right. Lesedi had relayed how his mum had called her and told her how much it would mean for him and for them as a family, if she could join them for the family get-away. She had told her she was aware of her family tradition for the holidays, and respected it. She only wanted to let her know that they loved her so much, and she was family to them, and they'd like very much if she considered them her family as well.

Lesedi told him how when she was about to drop the phone, when his mother had told her, "Oh, and from one woman to another, my son really likes you, he is just shy". They both laughed as Khaya tried to deny being shy. "I wasn't shy the other day at the beach was I?" Khaya protested. "Oh yes, you were. I was the bold one, remember?" And what kind of a man sends his mother to do his bidding anyway?" She asked as she chased him around the room. He thanked his mother for stepping in, but told her that he now had to repair the damage to his ego. His mother told him he was welcomed, and wanted to know if they had anything planned for the day. He sat down on the bed, and told the mother he actually needed her advice.

Lesedi had forgotten how beautiful Aniston's shorelines were, as they walked hand in hand, barefooted, to the cave. They discussed her applications to GS and Bellville Hospital for the position of a registered nurse. He prayed that she would get one of the positions so she could move back to Cape Town. He also planned to get his own place as soon he was able to get a suitable place in town, close to work. She asked if he had told his parents about his plans to move out. He told her he was still waiting for the perfect time. He was scared of hurt their feelings. Maybe if he had a very good reason, one that they couldn't dispute, it wouldn't be so bad.

Lesedi held her breath. The sight of the cliffs was mind-blowing. Khaya held her hands as they maneuvered across the rocks along the edges of the cliff, and through the narrow rocky entrance to the cave. She looked around in amazement as they stepped into the 'lobby'. She couldn't believe she had missed such a beautiful treasure all this while.

Khaya held her hand, "Remember that good reason I spoke about earlier for moving out of my parent's house?" He asked. "I think I may have just found one. What if we got engaged?" He added, as he reached into his pocket, bringing out a gold ring.

Lesedi was speechless. Did she just hear him right? Was he asking her to marry him, and where did he get a ring from? A million thoughts ran through her mind in a matter of seconds as she tried to process what she just heard.

He reached for her left hand and slid the ring into her fourth finger. It was a little loose, but it didn't matter. He would sort that out later. She stared at the ring on her finger, still reeling from the shock of the moment. "Did you plan this along? Where did you get the ring from?" She asked. He told her he hadn't planned it. It just occurred to him that there couldn't be a more perfect time. The ring was his mum's—she had lent it to him and wanted her to have it if she wanted to.

She was thrilled beyond words. It wasn't how she had imagined he'd propose, but she wouldn't have it any other way. This was way better. She embraced him as tears rolled down her cheek. She loved him so much and couldn't think of any other person she'd rather spend the rest of her life. It was the best day of her life.

"But now, white boy, you have to get your parents to call my parents, so they can start the whole negotiation thing you know. Oh, they may need help from your other relatives. Maybe you want to call Aunty Nosfundo, uh?" She said, bursting into laughter. "Really? Are we doing the whole...?" Khaya quipped. "Yes, darling! We are doing this my way!" She chided, looking straight at him with her hands on her hip. He nodded quickly in agreement as he led her out of the cave.

"Get the cattle ready, *Monna ke eng*?" Lesedi said, with a smirk on her face.

It was a very rainy December in Cape Town the year of their wedding. The church was filled to capacity, in spite of the rain. Khaya looked at Bayo, his best man. He looked exhausted. He couldn't blame him. It had been a busy two weeks since he arrived in the country. He could tell he was relieved that they were almost at the end of the two week marathon of wedding activities.

Khaya felt a sudden frisson of excitement and nervousness as the customary procession song 'Here comes the bride...' filtered through the speakers of the Anglican Diocese of Cape Town. He watched with fullness of joy, as his wife was led, hand in hand, into the church by her father. He could have sworn she winked at him, just as their eyes locked under her veil. She was always the cheery one.

He smiled to himself. It was a new beginning, a new opportunity to be happy. His eyes wondered around the big reception hall, relatives and friends—

217

and ancestors he was sure—were all gathered to celebrate the newly pronounced Mr and Mrs Khaya Johnson. Some had travelled with him to the Free State for their engagement and were now here with them in Cape Town. He was filled with gratitude.

He looked across to his parents. They smiled back at him. His speech earlier had been all about them. They epitomised a love that transcended colour. He had reminded them that the day was as much, theirs. He wanted them to know that he would always make them proud, and that they now have another daughter in Lesedi. He looked at the room one more time. He was proud of himself and glad that he found his way back home, to those he truly cared about and who cared about him too. This experiencing love, was his true identity, and he learnt to embrace it.

———

Khaya ran after the three elderly women, but something was different, he could see the shadow of another woman ahead of them. It looked like Mammi. He cried out to her, but she didn't look at him. Khaya kept crying out until the women were almost disappearing into the shadows and then suddenly, she turned around, there was a big smile on her face. It was her. He ran towards the dwindling image but all he could hear was, "*Jonghikaya, ndiyakuthanda mntwana wami* (Jonghikaya, I love you my child)". "I love you too, Mammi!" He cried out.

Lesedi, who was awake most of the night, watched in utter amazement, as her new husband wriggled, moaned and mumbled away in his dream. She wondered if she hadn't underestimated his demons!

Epilogue

It was the summer of 2001. Khaya's mother had just turned sixty. They planned a small gathering of family and close friends to celebrate the milestone. It was also the year of Khaya's fifth wedding anniversary. It was a reminder of how far they had come as a family.

Khaya and family decided to stay for the rest of the weekend. The kids were always happy to spend time with their grandparents in beautiful Aniston. Except it had been cloudy since they arrived on Friday— the sky was overcast which made going to the beach unappealing.

Saved by the weather, he had been on the losing end of the monopoly game when the kids ran to the patio to notify them that the sky had suddenly cleared. They pointed in childish gesture, to a slight ray of sunlight shining through the clouds. "Daddy, let's go", they chorused. They looked so cute. It was hard to deny them such joy, so Khaya gave in. He could never understand their unwavering love for the sea. Not that he minded, he always enjoyed swimming in warm seas.

Exhausted from multiple rounds of volley ball, Khaya laid buried under the sand. He heard the ground vibrate around him. Fearing that an earthquake may be unfolding, he scrambled to get out from the sand dunes his daughter had built around him. But it was his phone vibrating. Khaya dusted off more sand from his clothes. He reached for it, dropping his pants with the rest of their stuff on the mat. It was an email notification.

He slowly sunk back onto the mat, completely taken aback by the email preview. He had not heard from her since he left the States. He opened up the message, and as he read on, it felt like the mythological zombies had just burst out from the ground below, into the present. Then another mail popped up. The image of a child loaded as he opened the message. He stared at the image, trembling, just as he heard a familiar voice behind him. It was his daughter. She peeped at his phone, "Who is she daddy? I want curly hair like that too", she added. He got up quickly, tucked the phone underneath his pants, and lifted her up on his shoulders. "No one baby, no one," he told her.

Lesedi and his son were moving closer. She had caught the look on his face the moment he had first opened up the email. She recognised the look. It was the same look he had when he had found his mother's notes.

He scooped up his son in time to avoid him crashing into his groin, while also enduring the pain from his daughter's nails as they gripped his skull to hold herself steady.

"Daddy magnet," Lesedi smiled as she caught up with them. "Is everything okay?" She asked. "Of course, everything's good." He avoided her gaze as they ran towards the beautiful warm sea.

www.ingramcontent.com/pod-product-compliance
Lightning Source LLC
Chambersburg PA
CBHW031100020726
47495CB00007B/1966